WHAT PEOPLE ARE S

COLLECTING F

Collecting Feathers transports us to a world where our mental barriers and overly constructed stories no longer reduce our existence. It opens a door to another dimension where imagination and reality collide, liberating us from our self-inflicted limitations. Daniela Norris exposes gracefully in this brief but powerful collection of short stories, how we are all connected, and how without judgement, evaluation, or labels, we are capable of accessing the greatest power of our Universe.
Sophie Parienti, Founder & Editor in Chief, *Yogi Times*

Like an interesting doorway into a secret inner garden, Daniela Norris' stories invite you into a rich experience of strange and fascinating personal culture. Before you know it, you find yourself on the other side of familiar boundaries of this life and what is beyond.
Mark Perry, CCHT, C-NLP - educator, healer, life fulfillment coach, and host of "A Matter of the Mind" radio show.

The settings of the eleven stories of *Collecting Feathers* are scattered around the globe – Africa, the Swiss Alps, Canada, Paris, South America... – but there are no real borders to these tales that cross our planet and stray between this world and the next. "Life is full of cycles," says the old woman in 'A Reason to Go On' and it doesn't matter that she is addressing a suicidal banker in Paris, as her words would be understood just as well by Iolanda who visits the grave of her nameless firstborn son on the Day of the Dead, Laurent who meets the ancient travelers of Curmilz, or Sarah as she shops at Trader Joe's. The names may change, the story details differ, but family ties and loyalty remain stronger than death and "truth is beyond words".

Gwyneth Box, Poet and Poetry coordinator, SWWJ

Most of us know 'life on the other side' only as a phrase. Daniela Norris shows considerable experience of this mysterious dimension, and shares it through her characters' everyday existences. The naturalness of her viewpoint captivates and she never blinks.

Wallis Wilde-Menozzi, author of *Toscanelli's Ray, a novel*

Daniela Norris is a writer of subtle intelligence. While her stories seldom have a twist, each tale has the power to wriggle out from under the readers' expectations.

Jason Donald, author of *Choke Chain, a novel*

Collecting Feathers

Tales from The Other Side

Collecting Feathers

Tales from The Other Side

Daniela I. Norris

Winchester, UK
Washington, USA

First published by Soul Rocks Books, 2014
Soul Rocks Books is an imprint of John Hunt Publishing Ltd., Laurel House, Station Approach,
Alresford, Hants, SO24 9JH, UK
office1@jhpbooks.net
www.johnhuntpublishing.com
www.soulrocks-books.com

For distributor details and how to order please visit the 'Ordering' section on our website.

Text copyright: Daniela I. Norris 2014

ISBN: 978 1 78279 671 8

A CIP catalogue record for this book is available from the British Library.

Design: Stuart Davies
www.stuartdaviesart.com

Printed and bound by CPI Group (UK) Ltd, Croydon, CR0 4YY

We operate a distinctive and ethical publishing philosophy in all
areas of our business, from our global network of authors to
production and worldwide distribution.

CONTENTS

A Reason to Go On

We saw storms in the eyes of the other patients. They stared at us enviously as we walked away on that grey, miserable morning. Could they have seen us both? We were the ones getting out, they were staying behind. Or was it the other way round?

"*Au revoir*, Olivier!" said the night-watchman, who was drinking his morning coffee at the nurses' station. His dark, furry cap looked like a rare animal curled up on his head, winking at me with its beady button eyes. I winked back. The night-watchman winked at me and smiled. Little did he know that the furry animal on his head had thoughts of its own, and they were not happy ones.

"Take care, Olly," said the blonde nurse who'd just arrived for her morning shift.

I'd been waiting for that day for eleven months, ever since being admitted to Saint Mande's. Eleven months of reflection, of looking around me and inside me. What did I find, what found me? The dark shadows that lurked in my head when I first arrived now hid in my liver, in my kidneys, in my joints and under my skin. They hid where they could not be seen by others, but I knew they were there. They refused to leave my body; or perhaps it was I who refused to let them go.

It had been a year with no visitors. I watched the winter snow melt into trickles of chocolate-vanilla streams that followed me everywhere. I was careful not to step on them, not to interrupt their flow. Then the bare trees started blooming in delight, bathing in the cold April sun, its teeth as prickly as a puppy's. It warmed the back of my neck as I sat on my favorite bench, waiting for the guests that never arrived. I watched the others as they strolled in the gardens or shared hot tea and a bun with their visitors in the lounge, which looked as if it belonged to a different era. So did those who sat in it, frozen smiles on their lips, cobwebs in their hair.

Truth be told, I did not mind being on my own. I surrendered to the calming presence that filled the large rooms, swirled around the white walls and brushed the high ceilings with the gentlest touch. I could hear the early summer winds whistling their melancholic tunes, accompanied by the sound of a distant piano. They whistled at me, for me. No one else seemed to hear them. Whoosh, whoosh, they would say, and I whooshed back at them, ignoring the loud protests of the starlings which must have been trying to distract me.

Of course I had hallucinations; it was the medication they insisted I take. They said it would calm me down, sooth my nerves, ease my strain.

It may have soothed my nerves, but it did things to my mind. It made me see patterns on those white walls, shapes forming, growing, taking over; creeping in and out, like the woman in Charlotte Perkins Gilman's "Yellow Wallpaper". Mine, like hers, was a temporary nervous depression. Like her, I was prescribed tonics, and journeys, and air, and exercise. And I was forbidden to work until I was well again.

Only now that I'd been declared healthy and mentally sane, at least sane enough to walk the streets, I started worrying about the future. I would be part of the community again. Would they care for me? Did I care for them when I was an all-mighty banker, drinking my *macchiato* in a paper cup, walking past those sitting on the sidewalk looking as if their world had just crumbled? I did give them a coin every now and then, feeling that I'd done my good deed for the day. But most of the time I drifted past them without giving them a second thought, and if I did think about why they were sitting there, I always assumed something was wrong with them. Perhaps they'd lost their minds.

I discovered that temporary insanity was indeed a good shield against life's difficulties and responsibilities – not that I am a man who avoids responsibility. After all, I'd followed the right path to success, the very same path my parents had skillfully laid out for me: a *grande école*, a well-paying job, marriage to a beautiful woman with perfect skin. And then it all crumbled when she left. Or perhaps it was the sixty-hour work weeks I had spent at my corner office at the *Place de Marché St. Honoré*, for in my previous life I was a self-importance-filled third-generation banker, wearing stripy suits and drinking chilled champagne to seal multi-million-euro deals.

Perhaps the loneliness was to blame. I had no real friends before, and certainly no real friends after. Of course there were my colleagues who were always happy to go for a drink after work. I can remember nights when we drank ourselves to stupor and stumbled back in the small hours of the morning. I would find her weeping in our bed, and then the bed was empty. I discovered how a stream of wealthy, inflated, stripy-suited executives can turn into a trickle of unhappy souls. Those who had no one to go back to, like myself, stayed out all night, or found an occasional partner. We didn't want to return to four empty walls. Those walls were always in some chic part of town, but it didn't make them less desolate.

These were no friends. They drank my chance of

happiness on the rocks, with a little colored umbrella. They shrugged in sympathy when I turned to be one of them, and then left me behind in search of their own happiness. That was before; after was worse.

After my suicide-attempt there were only whispers around me, no one courageous enough to tell me I was throwing my life into the recycling bin.

They all seemed to have forgotten I'd ever existed, and my corner office was given to another hotshot who would probably drift in a similar path to mine.

I don't remember when I had a real friend, if I ever had one. But then I noticed him staring at me from behind a tree in the garden, and I felt he was different. He brought a smile to my face and interest to my soul at a time when nothing else seemed to make a difference.

He made me feel less isolated; he encouraged me with a thin smile or with a wave of a hand. Sometimes I knew he was near me before I even turned to see him. He became a part of my life, as much as the dozen small, round tablets I took every morning, the watery coffee at the *canteen* and the daily therapy sessions with Dr. Gerard, the resident psychiatrist.

This companion, this improbable friend, was a young man about my age; he followed me silently wherever I went. He never said a thing to me; I never said a thing to him. He was so quiet, so discreet, no one else noticed him.

He used to loiter around the garden; I could see him through the bars on my window when I gazed outside at the meticulous lawn. Gilman's garden was 'delicious, full of box-bordered paths, and lined with long grape-covered arbors with seats under them'. Mine was scrupulous. Just the sight of this perfect lawn could drive someone mad, but they didn't care. In their eyes, we were all crazy anyway. They didn't care when I walked along the straight, graveled paths, one foot before the other, my arms up to keep my balance. And since they didn't mind, I didn't either. It felt good to be childlike, to do things that a respectable man in his thirties would never dream of doing.

He thought it was funny, and I could sometimes see him rolling with laughter at my childish pranks. He understood that I needed to let it all out, let the reins of control loose before I was ready to pick them up again and ride into the sunset.

Sometimes my friend appeared unannounced, peeking from behind bookshelves when I was reading in the small library or waiting patiently for my therapy sessions. He never got very close, which was just as well. It was a time in my life where I didn't handle closeness well. He must have sensed that, as he always kept his distance, hovering around me in his own invisible pattern.

I did mention my friendly stalker to Dr. Gerard once; the only thing he did was increase my medication. So I never mentioned him again.

After they finally took me off the anti-depressants, he didn't appear as often. I spent a lot of time walking around in the vast gardens, on my own, looking for him behind every tree, seeking his slender figure in the shadows of the old, glorious buildings.

On those solitary strolls, thoughts of the shame I'd caused my family started trickling into my mind. It is shame, rather than pain that I had caused, as all of their self-indulgent, pretentious friends had heard about my suicide attempt through the Parisian social grapevine, and must have clucked in disbelief over their *fois-gras* and expensive wine. As much as my parents tried to sweep the incident under their Persian rug, sending me to *Saint Mandé* in a straitjacket as soon as I was released from hospital, it was no use. Everyone knew.

They visited me twice over the past year – once on my birthday, and once the day before Christmas. Father said Dr. Gerard had told them not to come. That their presence upset me. But neither their presence, nor the lack of it, interfered with my plans.

"Can I take that for you?" asked the taxi driver, pointing to my black suitcase. He threw it in the trunk and shut it with a slam.

"Where to, *Monsieur*?" he wanted to know, looking at me in the rearview mirror. His eyebrows were like two hairy caterpillars. They made me think of the earthworms I used to collect in a tin can on the summers I'd spent with my grandparents in Brittany, in their old house. The house always smelt of my grandmother's baking, of sweet butter and almond biscuits that crumbled on the instant they touched my tongue, and turned into a small mash of heaven. I used to hold each bite in my mouth, hold it until I had to swallow only because I needed to open my mouth to breathe and then ate another and another until Grandmother would slap my wrist and take the biscuit tin away from me. Just the thought of those biscuits made me salivate all these years after the last crumb had melted away into a distant memory.

It's been so many years since I've been to that old house, which was renovated by Father to accommodate the distinguished company he invited there, to show off his real 'deep France' roots. There was no more place for me in that house, my childhood memories wiped off with a few strokes of a brush. Was there a place for me anywhere now?

I hesitated. There was nowhere in the world I wanted to go. But I didn't want to remain at the institution either.

The taxi driver shifted uncomfortably in the front seat, looking as if he was having second thoughts about taking this fare. I suppose it wasn't every day that he was driving a patient from a mental institution, and he probably wasn't sure about the protocol. He then decided to wait, cleaning the steam our breaths had created on the front windshield with his gloved fingers.

I reluctantly gave him the address of my old apartment, as I could think of nowhere else to go. It was right in the center of the 15th *arrondissement,* above a Nicolas wine store and an antique furniture boutique. My father had been paying the rent for the past year. He didn't want me to lose it and end up on the streets, or worse, back at my parents' house, where I would put them all to shame again.

The driver started the car and I sank back in my seat, taking in the gloomy early winter morning through the tinted window, wishing I were someone else, someone who knew where their life was going. The drive through the busy streets of Paris brought back the longing I was so familiar with before the incident; some of that dangerous, desperate loneliness that got its grip on me just before I had attempted to slash my veins in my parents' guest bathroom.

They were awfully upset about the mess I'd made of the *artisanal* sink, a unique piece from the 1930s with golden fish taps that were gasping for air, their mouths wide open and their eyes two black dots staring with rage. They looked at me with such evil eyes, they knew what I was up to, and if they could speak I am sure they would have called my parents in loud fishy squeaks. With a vengeance, I scraped off their golden-plated scales before I proceeded to scrape my own wrists. That would teach them a lesson.

After the incident, everyone whispered around me; they all talked in low voices, as if there was someone dying. My parents didn't ask why I did it. They just assumed I had gone mad. And I did not have the inclination to correct their assumptions, as that would be as if I was admitting that their assumptions mattered.

Dr. Gerard asked if I really wanted to die, and I said that I supposed that if I really wanted to die I would have been dead by now. There are not many things I wanted in life and did not get, which is why not getting what I wanted had put me off balance, concluded Dr. Gerard. I disagreed.

As we stopped at the red light on Boulevard Diderot, just outside the magnificent *Gare de Lyon* train station, I saw him. There was no doubt it was him.

He stood at the bus stop, about thirty yards from me. His red scarf was wrapped around his neck to keep him warm; his hands were deep in the pockets of his leather jacket, similar to the one I was wearing. He waved the fringe of his red scarf at me; I felt as if I was the bull and he was the *matador*, waving the red cloth in front of my eyes. He smiled mischievously.

"Stop!" I hollered, my voice hoarse and unfamiliar. The taxi driver turned around, frightened, and stared at me with horrified eyes. He wanted to make sure I wasn't about to jump on him from behind and strangle him, or do some other unexplainable act you'd kind of expect from an ex-banker turned madman.

When he saw that my attention was focused on the bus stop outside and not on his throat, he sighed with relief and swung out of the creeping traffic at once, stopping by the sidewalk.

I threw some money at him and sprang out of the car like a cork out of a bottle of champagne, grabbing my suitcase from the trunk even before it was completely open. The driver didn't dare come out, and after popping the boot from inside the taxi he sat there frozen, staring at the rearview mirror in disbelief.

My mysterious friend was no longer at the bus stop. Was he a figment of my imagination? Perhaps I *was* as unwell as they all claimed. Was this an omen, maybe some kind of curse? Or was madness clutching me in its velvety claws, trying to tempt me to follow it to the end of reality. Was my mind really playing tricks on me?

But no, now I could see his dark head floating fifty yards ahead, slipping away through the crowd. A low hum, a kind of murmur resonated in my ears. I realized it was the magnified tapping of hundreds of leather soles on the sidewalk, the white noise of mobile phones ringing and people shooting meaningless words into them. It washed over me like a ripple, in slow motion.

I followed the dark head, determined not to lose it in the crowd. But then he disappeared. I strained my eyes, but he was gone.

I collapsed on a seat inside the *Gare de Lyon*, a splendid edifice built for the World Exposition of 1900. Over my head, giant boards flickered, displaying the comings and goings of trains to different destinations. Lyon, Dijon, Grenoble, Geneva.

I dropped my head in my hands and wept. After the long months of solitude, the prospect of struggling through life alone, was terrifying. I used to have a supporting partner, a loving family. Now I had no one. It was too much to bear.

Someone sat down next to me with a thump, sighing loudly. Something brushed against my sleeve. Was it a pickpocket trying to steal my wallet? What difference would it make if it were? Earthly possessions were the last thing on my mind.

"Are you all right, dear?" whispered a voice in my ear. I didn't move, didn't look up. *Can't they see that I'm unwell? Why don't they just let me be?*

Someone tugged at my sleeve. I raised my head and stared straight into the violet eyes of an elderly lady. She looked exhausted. The large bag at her feet touched my shoes, and I moved my feet.

"*Pardon*," she said. "Sorry. I just wanted to make sure you are all right."

Why would she care if I was all right or not? Wasn't it obvious I wasn't?

I looked at her silently, brushing my eyes with the back of my hand, to wipe any traces of tears. My eyes were dry. I no longer cried with tears, as if my tear-ducts had dried up.

She smiled at me. I noticed her face was wrinkled and dry, but her eyes clear and warm. I said nothing.

"I am sorry," she repeated.

I shrugged and dropped my head back in my hands. I felt safe in this position, the cruel world hidden from my eyes.

She sighed again, a deep, slow moan that resonated in my own chest and forced me to look up again.

"It's not easy to be alone," she said. "This was my last trip. I am not doing this again."

We sat there in silence, two strangers in a bubble of joint sorrow, pain that radiated outwards through the pores of our skins and rode the tide of our breaths, making them shallow and stale.

She sighed one final time, as if she had given up, and stood on her feet, supporting herself on a walking cane. She struggled to lift her bag, an old-fashioned, beaten-up leather case. In another life, I would have offered to help her. But now, now it didn't feel as if I could help anyone; not even myself.

"Can I help you?" the words slipped out of my mouth. I had no intention of saying them. It was as if my former self, the sociable, kind, life-loving man had surfaced, taking over the shaking, pitiful shadow of a man I now was, for a fraction of a moment. She looked at me, surprised. Now that I'd said the words, a new energy rushed into my body. Why was I offering to help her? Maybe because she looked even lonelier and sadder than me. Or maybe because she didn't know anything about my past. She didn't treat me as if I was an important young executive, nor did she treat me as if I was a madman. I didn't know how to be anything other than these two people, the only two people I had ever been – and no longer was.

I jumped to my feet, grabbing my own suitcase in my left hand and extending my right towards the elderly lady. She hesitated, but my smile convinced her and she handed me her bag with trembling hands. I noticed she was elegantly dressed, pearl earrings in her lobes and a matching pearl brooch on the lapel of her jacket. These were clothes from another time in her life, I thought, a time when she was invited to silver-wedding-anniversary parties and to afternoon teas.

Now she walked by my side in slow steps, her head at the level of my shoulder, her white hair pinned at the back of her head in a bun. She led me through the station, down the stone steps and back onto the bustling avenue I'd just left a few minutes before in chase of a fickle phantom.

I noticed that the sun had come through the clouds; not the hungry, cruel sun with sharp teeth that had shone on me just the day before, but a different sun, with a million stroking, gentle arms. The soft light bathed the grey streets around me in yellow dust. It wasn't such a despondent day after all.

"I live just a few blocks away," said the elderly lady. "You don't have to come the whole way."

I didn't answer. I just kept walking, my eyes staring ahead. She tried again.

"You don't have to carry it all the way, it's all right," she said softly. The compassion in her voice seemed to penetrate the armor that surrounded me and made its way to my ears, the ears that were now accustomed to filtering human voices as if they were grains of rock in flowing water.

"I'll accompany you," I said, or maybe whispered, and she touched the sleeve of my leather jacket in what must have been a gesture of gratitude. I was beginning to feel like a human being again.

What did she see when she looked at me? I wondered. A man in his early thirties, dressed in jeans and a black leather jacket, stubble on his face, sadness in his eyes. I was once a handsome man, but now my cheeks were sunken and my soul was filled with emptiness, which I was sure that anyone looking in my eyes could see. But no one looked me in the eye these days. I seemed to have become invisible.

Now this lady noticed me. She smiled at me again, a kind smile that had neither pretensions, nor secret intentions. But what else was in her eyes? I thought I could see speckles of concern. Could she possibly know that I had a plastic bag full of sleeping pills, accumulated over the past months in a dirty sock in my bag?

"A handsome man like you shouldn't look so dispirited," she said, and stopped for a moment of rest.

I considered my response. What could I say? I needed to find something that wouldn't be a lie, but wouldn't be the complete truth either, because the truth would scare her away.

"I'm much better than I was a few months ago," I finally said, avoiding her eyes.

She resumed walking in small, slow steps, and I paced by her side. My duffle bag was over my left shoulder, her beat-up leather case dangling in my right. It was strange that I felt as if she was the one doing me a favor, walking by my side on the streets that were full of people coming from somewhere, heading somewhere else. They all knew where they were going. All, except for me. Had any of them ever walked without purpose, without knowing where they were going or why? This was a new experience for me, because in a previous life I had always led the way. It was strange to be on the other side of life now, as if I was looking at all these people through a one-way mirror. I could see them all but they didn't see me. I could read their minds, and they looked right through me.

We crossed the street, turned right on *rue de Charenton* and she pointed to an iron gate twenty yards ahead.

"That's where I live," she said. "Thank you. Can I pay you for your kind assistance?"

I shook my head and put her bag down by the gate. I didn't need her money. Money was never an issue in my family, and even now, after months of absence, I had no doubt that my father had made sure my bank-account was nicely padded. It was much easier for him to make a bank transfer than to hug me.

"I don't want money," I said. I didn't know what else to say, but there were still things that were left unsaid. I wished she'd invite me inside, into her home, offer me a biscuit. I hoped she'd take me in like a lost puppy she'd found on the street. If she said goodbye now, where would I go?

She narrowed her clear violet eyes and looked at me with concentration, as if trying to determine whether I was a potential serial killer. Then she made up her mind.

"How about a cup of tea?" she asked. "If you're not in a hurry."

I wasn't in a hurry. I didn't wait for her to ask a second time – I accepted without ceremony. Departing from a previous life to a new one is like waking up on the sidewalk with all your belongings scattered around you. You can't be a chooser, but you certainly don't want to become a beggar. So I pretended I was the one doing her a service, carrying her heavy bag.

I followed her up the stairs, stopping every few moments so she could catch her breath. We reached the third floor; I stood awkwardly before the apartment's heavy wooden door, shifting my weight from one foot to the other, while she rummaged in her bag.

She finally pulled out a large key and inserted it in the lock. It was stiff, and she turned it twice with some effort.

While she boiled water for tea in her small kitchenette, I sat down in an armchair in her front room and looked around. The room was bright, with two long windows that looked onto the street beneath us. A tall ceiling with moldings around the edges and furniture that was older than me gave the impression that time stood still. The sofa, covered with a once-golden fabric, was now matte with age and heavy with memories. A small rug, I could see it was a Persian, lay at my feet. I turned the corner up and peeked underneath, but if there was any shame there, it was well-hidden.

I looked around for photographs of grandchildren, of family. The only photograph in the room was displayed in the center of the mantelpiece, in a silver frame. I stood up and tiptoed towards it, so I could have a better look.

In it was my host, her face much smoother, her eyes much happier. She stood between two men. It looked as if they'd had a walk on the beach on a windy autumn day – the three of them wore windbreakers and scarves, but no hats. The man on her left was in his late forties or early fifties, the man on her right in his mid-twenties. The three of them were standing on the beachfront, the wind blowing in their hair, waves breaking behind them in fury. They smiled at the camera and had their arms around each other's shoulders. The young man looked disturbingly familiar.

I could hear her steps approaching from the kitchen, and slunk back from the photograph. I stuck my hands in my pockets and looked down, trying not to appear as if I was snooping around. She smiled genially and carried a small tray into the room. She laid it on the center of the table, and carefully removed two flowery Coalport porcelain cups with matching saucers and arranged them with slow, careful motions. It was clear from her body language that she hadn't had guests in a long time.

She walked back to her kitchen and returned with a box of chocolates, which looked as ancient as the furniture. She must have had it for quite a while, but waited for a special occasion to open it. I was the special occasion, which felt strange. It had been ages since I was anyone's special occasion.

She served me, then herself, and sat down heavily in one of the two armchairs. I collapsed in the second. I must have stared at the picture again, and she followed my gaze.

"My husband and my son," she said. "Both dead."

"I'm sorry," I said and meant it. I really did feel sorry for her.

She sighed.

"It's been a while now. Fifteen years, to be precise," she said.

We sat there in silence for a moment or two. Then she continued, talking to herself as much as she talked to me. She didn't look directly at me, but stared at the picture and addressed her words to it. I guessed she did this quite often.

"My son took his own life. And my husband died

shortly after. He couldn't cope with our son's death."

I sat motionless in the comfortable armchair, as if I was in a womb of fabric and wood. I waited for her to continue, and sipped the sweet dark tea she served in the fine china cup.

"He was thirty-three when he died," she said after a few moments of silence.

"I turned thirty-three last month," I said.

She looked at me with wonder and nodded silently, as if I said something she'd heard before.

"You look a lot like him," she said. What could I say to that? I nodded.

I wanted to ask how he died, but I didn't, because I feared the answer. There had been many questions turning in my mind for months now. How do people die? What was the best way to die? What was the difference between different kinds of deaths? If one chose one way of death over another, could they feel regret at their very last moment, regret on the kind of death they are dying, perhaps wishing it was a different kind?

"He took sleeping pills," she said, as if reading my mind. "Three days passed before his *concierge* found him in his apartment. We disagreed on many things, and were not very close in his last few years. We hardly spoke to him or saw him. I'll never forgive myself."

She didn't seem to feel uncomfortable talking about this with a man she just met. In fact, it was almost as if she'd been waiting to talk, as if it gave her some relief.

"Why did he do it?" I asked, truly wanting to know.

She shrugged, and took a deep breath. She held it in for what seemed like forever, and then let it out in another one of those deep, long sighs of hers.

"Who knows? I can only imagine what went through his head. He wasn't very well. Wasn't well at all in his last couple of years."

"Still," I said. "There must be a reason."

This was the first real conversation I had had in over a year, and I wasn't about to give it up. It made me feel alive, part of the real world again. It reminded me that other people had problems. And she did seem to want to pursue this as much as I did. After all, she was the one who invited me in. I wanted to know what had happened to her son. I needed to know. His story touched a familiar chord inside me, perhaps it was the answer to a question I always wanted to ask but never dared.

She spoke in a slow, hoarse voice, as if she was playing the strings of a musical instrument that had lain silent for many years.

"His wife left him; then he started drinking. He was in a terrible state. Then, of course, he lost his job. He was heart-broken. I don't blame his wife for any of it – he was not an easy man to live with. He was never around. Too involved in his important work. She wanted a family, he didn't feel up for it. When she left and returned to America, he just drank and drank. He may have taken drugs as well, I don't know. What I do know is that we were not around to support him when he needed us. We didn't know how to cope with his personality change, with his illness."

She paused and poured some more tea into my cup. I didn't even notice I was clutching it, clinging to it as if it could solve all my problems, all of her problems.

"He spent a few months in a hospital, at *Saint Mandé*. When he was released, he went back to his apartment and took sleeping pills he'd collected during his stay there."

I shifted uncomfortably in my armchair as I thought of the collection of sleeping pills I'd accumulated in the sock, hidden in the small inside pocket of my blue bag.

"I just got out of *Saint Mandé*, less than an hour ago," I

whispered.

She looked at me with her clear velvet eyes, the clouds in her irises slowly drifting away. She shook her head.

"How curious," she said. "How very strange."

She thought about it for a moment or two, and then smiled at me, as if she'd reached a conclusion.

"Life is full of cycles," she said. "You know, I can't help thinking that maybe, if we had been more attentive all those years ago, he would be alive today."

"You shouldn't blame yourself," I whispered once more, thinking of my own parents. Would they mourn if I were gone, mourn my death like this lady had been mourning the death of her son over the past fifteen years? I couldn't help wondering.

"I no longer blame myself," she continued, her voice breaking up, but her eyes dry and hard. "I did for many years. When my husband died, I thought about ending it all myself, but I didn't. I continued living, because I was stronger than them, stronger than both of them. Hearts heal if you give them time, you know."

"Doesn't feel like it sometimes," I said.

"The only thing we can all be sure of, is that we will die some day. We might as well take advantage of what life has to offer us," she said. There was a compassionate look in her eyes. I could see she was trying to be cheerful, but this conversation was as hard for her as it was for me. Perhaps even harder.

I didn't know what to else to say, and she kept quiet for some minutes. Then she surrendered to the drowsiness that covered us both like a blanket, a drowsiness caused by the stillness in the air and the warm, dry central heating. I watched as her eyelids closed slowly and her chin touched her collarbone.

I placed my tea cup on the table, careful not to make a

sound. I was just about to get up and look at the photograph again, when the bedroom door opened and a young man walked in. It was him. It was definitely him. The hairs on the back of my neck stood like wooden toothpicks. He nodded in greeting and confidently sat down on the faded sofa.

"My mother always does this, no disrespect to you," he said. He took his slippers off and stretched his legs. "She gets very tired lately."

Was I dreaming? Nothing I could say felt appropriate. It was the first time I heard his voice, and it was exactly as I imagined it would be. Calm, low, very familiar.

He didn't seem to mind my silence and was quite content just sitting there, gazing at me and at his sleeping mother with clear, almost hypnotizing, eyes. He didn't look much older than he was in the photograph on the mantelpiece. Somewhat older, perhaps, more lines around the eyes, but certainly not in his forties, as he should have been according to my calculations.

"So…what are you doing here?" I asked, feeling stupid as the question left my lips.

"I am looking after my mother. She hasn't been well lately. Besides, I wanted to talk to you. It's been a while now, hasn't it?"

It was as if his words confirmed my worst suspicions, my unthinkable fears. I was surely not talking to a ghost. It must be the other option then; I was truly losing it.

"How did you know I was here?" I bit my lips as another silly question left them.

He looked at me, amused. If he were a ghost he would know what I was thinking, wouldn't he? I didn't know very much about ghosts – not many ex-bankers do.

"I brought you here, didn't I?" he said and smiled. "At the hospital, when you first arrived, I felt for you. You really reminded me of myself, fifteen years back."

He waited for me to say something, but I had nothing to say, so he continued.

"Earlier today, when you got out, I was afraid you were going straight back to your apartment, so I tried to get your attention, to bring you somewhere where we could talk. And here you are now," he ended with a triumphant smile, as if he were waiting for applause. I was speechless.

"What can I do for you, then?" I asked after a few moments of silence.

"Well," he said, "since you're asking, I'll tell you. You were thinking of ending it anyway, weren't you?"

He looked straight at me, confident that I knew what he was talking about. Of course I did. There would be no point in trying to deny it, would there? I didn't think he would jump to his feet and call the police.

"Well, would you mind looking after my mother for a while?"

"Looking after your mother?" I asked, confused.

He nodded, and I waited for him to go on.

"I feel so guilty about not being here when she needs me. I thought perhaps you'd be able to help," he said and looked me in the eye, his face serious and hopeful.

I looked back at him, still baffled. He continued.

"My mother was diagnosed with a terminal illness last year, and she isn't going to live much longer. At least I'd like it to end nicely for her. She is a very lonely lady."

"What would you like me to do, then?" I asked, expecting clear instructions, some words that would put some sense into what he was trying to say.

"Just look after her, take her out every now and then. She never really goes out of the house, except for medical appointments. She took the last trip today, to my father's grave. He is buried near Dijon, that's where he was from, where he wanted to be buried. And when she dies, you'd still be free to choose, to decide what you want to do."

I was beginning to grasp his intention, his incomprehensible intention. If all he wanted was for me to spend some time with his ill mother, to give her a reason to go on a little longer, there was no cause for me to refuse. I could always die another day, there was no rush.

"I promise that whenever it is you show up on the other side, I'll be there to show you around," he said with one of those mischievous smiles I recognized by now. "It can be a bit confusing at first."

I didn't need more convincing; this sounded like a pretty good deal, if there was any grain of reality in it.

"Sure..." I said, not able to think of anything else to add. If this was for real, I'd be gaining here and there.

"I appreciate it," he said as he stood up, stepping back into his slippers. "Just don't mention it to my mother. It may upset her."

"Nice meeting you, finally," I said to the empty sofa. The old lady was standing in front of me, wearing a different cardigan. She looked as if she had time to freshen up after the trip.

"You dozed off," she said. "You must have slept for forty minutes or so. Would you like another cup of tea?"

"No thanks," I said, still a little confused. I stood up.

"I'd better head off. Would you mind if I kept in touch?" I asked.

She looked at me and smiled.

"It would be wonderful," she said.

"Maybe I can take you out for tea next week," I added.

"I'd love that," she said. "I must tell you, I probably won't be around for long, but please do call next week. It would be nice to see you again."

I noted down her telephone number and we parted with

a kiss on each cheek.

I headed for the bus that would take me to my old apartment. I felt strong enough to face the shadows I would find there. After all, now I had an obligation, a promise I had to fulfill. I had a reason to go on.

The Day of the Dead

He was born and died on November 1st, the Day of the Dead.

"It was an omen," said Iolanda.

"It was a curse," disagreed her older sister, Ezmeralda.

Iolanda nodded. Her heavy earrings jingled.

She was a large woman, her perfect skin glowing on her dark face like a full moon over distant fields, far from the city lights.

Every year, on her first son's birthday and death day, she went to visit his grave and lit a candle for his soul. She'd had four other children in the ten years that followed that afternoon when she gave birth to a small, shriveled baby. He took one breath and then gave his soul back to his creator, to the master of souls or to wherever souls come from.

"It is probably Antonio's first wife who put the curse," added Ezmeralda.

That sad afternoon the midwife came running, carrying her bag of herbal remedies and a handful of clean rags. She entered the small hut and encountered a pale, bleeding twenty-year-old in a mild state of shock.

Experienced with first-time mothers, the midwife set a plastic sheet on the hut's dirt floor and lay Iolanda on it. She wiped Iolanda's brow with a damp cloth and sent for her assistant, a fifteen-year-old apprentice girl living in the same village.

"This will be complicated," she said to Iolanda. "You

must keep your strength."

The screams that burst out of the little hut that afternoon made the women of the neighborhood gather around, asking if there was anything they could do to help. The midwife sent them all away.

"Everything will be fine," she said.

Everything wasn't fine. After twelve hours of bleeding and labor, a tiny creature emerged. His fists were clutched in rage and his face was wrinkled like an old man's. He didn't even scream. He took one breath and then went limp and lifeless in the midwife's hands. Iolanda never got to hold him.

The midwife sent her assistant to take care of the technicalities. A small grave was dug at the far end of the village where the dead were buried. The small body was covered in a clean sheet and buried that same day. In the tropical climate bodies could not be left outside in the heat but had to be buried straight away to avoid disease.

When Antonio returned from town that night he encountered a faint, pallid Iolanda with a hollow look in her eyes. He had to take her to hospital, for she'd lost so much blood she required a transfusion. The cost was outrageous but the neighbors from the village all chipped in and Iolanda got the best of the very limited medical treatment available.

She returned to her little hut three days later and resumed her daily chores. It wasn't until she became pregnant again five months later that she took the fifteen-minute walk to visit her firstborn's grave. She went to apologize for not coming before and for replacing him so soon.

In a country that had known years of civil war, a stillborn was not a tragedy. Tragedies happened every day in the interior with rebel forces butchering entire villages and burning whole towns. People disappeared, never to be seen again. Bodies were found in mass graves. A baby that didn't live to see the light of day did not leave a gap in anyone's heart – except for Iolanda's.

Her husband Antonio performed his duties in the years to come and brought food to their humble hut. He was a good man, even if he spent some of the money he earned in his job as a janitor in one of the crumbling government offices in town on other women and on drinks.

Iolanda considered herself lucky. She had her own hut to live in. She did not have to ask for any favors from her extended family and there was always some food on the table. Antonio also gave her four other children – all girls – and they helped her with the daily chores and selling the vegetables from her patch at the local market.

Yet, every year on the Day of the Dead, she bought a chicken at the market and prepared a slow-cooking, rich stew. She gathered flowers from a nearby field and made a small, pretty necklace, just the right size to fit around a baby's neck. She would never consider visiting her son without these offerings.

When her daughters were too young to walk she carried them on her back. When they were older, they followed her, offerings in hand, to the far end of the village to pay their respects to their older brother.

"How come our brother doesn't have a name, Mai?" asked Maria, the eldest.

"Because he didn't live to be named," said Iolanda.

Her hands were busy wiping the small stone that had only a date engraved in it. It was November 1st, 1979.

"Why only this day, Mai?" asked Isabela, the second daughter.

"It is the only day he ever knew," replied Iolanda.

"Why is it such a small grave?" asked Antonia, the third

daughter.

"He was very small when he died, much smaller than you are now," answered Iolanda.

"Where is he now?" asked Fernanda, the youngest.

"He is waiting for us in heaven," said Iolanda. Then she wiped her hands on her skirt, kissed the stone and gathered her daughters around her for the short journey back.

The Day of The Dead was the only day in the year that Iolanda visited her son's grave despite its proximity to her hut. But as the years went by, the connection with the memory of her son grew stronger and stronger.

Every now and then he would visit her in her dreams. He was always a little baby, still shriveled with the effort of coming through the birth canal but Iolanda knew what he was feeling. Sometimes he was grimacing, as if saying "I hope you have not stopped thinking of me, Mai."

Other times he would be content, his dark eyes shiny and calm.

She told the village elder woman about these dreams.

"Keep your ears open to the messages the dead send, my daughter, for they are real," was the advice she got.

So Iolanda started looking forward to these nocturnal encounters, waking up calm in the morning, although the gap in her heart never really healed.

She knew Antonio was disappointed not to have had another son and even suggested they try again. She was only thirty, and her wide, heavy hips were meant to bear children.

"We can't afford to feed another mouth," said Antonio. But Iolanda knew he meant that they couldn't afford to have another girl.

She couldn't stop wondering what it would have been like to put her little son to her breast, to give him a little taste of what life had to offer. Maybe he wouldn't have chosen to die.

Iolanda wiped her hands on her stained green skirt and wrung the wet laundry into a clean plastic container. Her eldest, Maria, was coming up the path towards the hut on her way back from school. Her dark-blue uniform skirt, normally sparkling clean, was covered in white dust.

"Look at you, girl. What happened to you?" asked Iolanda.

"I was called to the front of the class, to write a solution on the blackboard," said Maria.

Iolanda said nothing. She couldn't see the use of all this education. Would it help her daughter find a job cleaning houses in town? Would it help find a good husband? No. It would just put unrealistic ideas in her mind. And in a country like theirs, one had got to be realistic to survive.

Now, had she been a boy it would have been a different story.

Maria walked past her mother into the small kitchen for a tepid glass of water. She was saddened by her mother's lack of interest in her studies, in how she did at school. She was a smart girl and knew she had little chance of finishing school before she had to go out and work for a living. But she enjoyed it while it lasted. She had no doubt in her mind that if she were a boy, if she were her dead older brother, her mother's attitude would have been different.

She still accompanied her mother every year to her brother's grave on November 1st but it didn't mean anything to her. There were so many people around her who died – two cousins who lived in a distant province and got killed in the war; an uncle that served in the army and vanished. Neighbors. Parents of friends from school. Why be so bothered about a one-day-old baby who didn't live long enough to be named?

"Mai, you have four live daughters," Maria said to her

mother years later. "Aren't we more important?"

By then her mother was very old, over fifty. In a country where the average life expectancy for women was forty-eight, that was no small achievement.

Her mother had had a hard life, though she considered it a good one. She was relying on Maria in her old age. Maria had a job as a secretary in the office of an international aid agency. She spoke Portuguese and English and was appreciated by her employers. Her salary was not enormous but was enough to get her mother out of that little hut where she grew up and put her up in a small apartment in town near where Maria worked.

Her father, Antonio, left home years ago to live with a new woman. Maria never married, but had two children. Her mother looked after them when they were very young.

This was life in her country and it never occurred to Maria that things could be different. She considered herself lucky to have a family, two children, a good job, many friends. But there was something that always bothered her and it was only getting worse.

Every year, on November 1st, she had to get her mother onto the local taxi-bus that took her to her old village. It wasn't very far from the city but the journey took an hour as the taxi-bus constantly stopped on the side of the road to drop off passengers and to pick up new ones.

In the first years after her mother had moved to town, Maria accompanied her. Then she let her mother perform this ritual on her own. Now that her mother was losing her eyesight, she would have to accompany her again, in about a week, to the village cemetery.

"Mai, it happened such a long time ago. You are not well. Why is he so important?" she asked.

"He is waiting for me," answered Iolanda. "He mustn't

think I forgot him."

"He is dead, Mai. He has been for thirty years."

"He is waiting for me."

Maria couldn't be bothered to continue the argument. Besides, where she came from, daughters didn't argue with their elderly mothers.

The following week she took a day off work, helped her mother put on an elegant, bright-colored dress and a matching head wrap, and got into a taxi-bus with her.

The way to the village was familiar, although Maria hadn't taken it for the best part of ten years. The cars were smoky and the road busy and noisy. It was much narrower than Maria remembered it. On the side of the road women in brightly colored cloths sold bananas and oranges from dirty straw baskets. Old men were pulling mules behind them, both weighed down by the weight they were carrying. The mules carried small pieces of furniture, clothes and baskets of fruit or vegetables. The men carried their years.

After what seemed like forever the taxi stopped and the driver called the name of the village. Her mother slowly lifted herself from the back seat and Maria helped her out of the taxi-bus and took her arm. They made their way slowly into the village, greeted by abandoned huts and a few chickens running around looking sorry and starving.

"Everyone lives in the city nowadays," said Iolanda.

"There is no one here, Mai. It is abandoned. You never told me," gasped Maria.

"There are still a few old friends," said Iolanda.

They stopped and greeted each of the three friends who were still living in the village – old women living on their own in run-down huts. Their children had died in the war or left the country. It was not so difficult to get work across the ocean anymore.

Maria felt the dust mixing with tears in her throat and then rising to the corners of her eyes. The walk to the cemetery, which used to take them fifteen minutes, now took nearly an hour. They stood in front of the stone in silence. The date, November 1st, 1979, was hardly visible. Antonio had carved it in his own hand more than twenty years before.

Maria felt the tears running down her dusty cheeks and was baffled to see her mother smile. She took a small bottle of water out of her bag, but instead of taking a sip or offering one to Maria she poured it over the stone. It shone in the bright sunlight.

They didn't stay long by the grave. It was hot and they still had a long way back. They stopped for a glass of water in one of the huts that was still inhabited and made their way to the main road. Neither woman said a word on the way back to town. They were both exhausted when they arrived at Iolanda's little apartment.

"Thank you for accompanying me," said Iolanda. "You are a good daughter."

"I am glad I did, Mai. I should have come with you more often. I'll take you again next year," said Maria. Iolanda smiled and petted her daughter's head.

"I am tired," she said. "I will go to bed now."

The following year, Maria made her way back to the village, back to the grave, on her own.

Repent

He stopped in the middle of the street and stared, frozen, unaccustomed to the feeling of panic that washed over him. He closed his eyes, then opened them again. He was still standing in the middle of a small street in Luanda, ninety degrees south of the equator.

She was walking away from him, stooped like a branch desperately clinging to the trunk of an old tree, her straight skirt exposing thin, white ankles.

He followed her, finding it hard to walk as slowly as the old woman in front of him.

He wiped his brow with a sweaty wrist and cursed the heat. She was not in a hurry. She advanced slowly, step by step, a little bag hanging from her right arm. With her left she raised her cane and dropped it down again, with every step she took. It tapped every time it hit the sidewalk. Paulo was amazed he could make out the sound against the general commotion on the busy street.

Cars drove past, their exhaust pipes releasing grey smoke into the humid summer air. People pushed by on the sidewalk, their clothes sticking to their backs, their faces shiny with sweat.

The old woman continued on, unconcerned. Tap, tap, tap, he could hear her cane hitting the burning pavement.

What if she recognized him there, right in the middle of the busy street?

Something inside him desperately wanted to turn around and run. He should just let her disappear in the crowd; let her leave his life. But he couldn't – she was the key to all the bad things that happened to him lately. He had got a possible chance to fix it. He couldn't let it slip away.

He followed her to a quieter street, where tall trees gave shade, little protection from the fervor of the summer day. Her small handbag hung on her arm, so exposed, so tempting. It would be easy to grab it. He pushed the thought right out of his mind.

Since their last encounter, everything had gone wrong in his life. His girlfriend left him for his best friend. Only days later he was caught by the police and spent a month in prison for picking the pocket of an elderly man. The elderly man was the father of an important clerk in the local administration, and Paulo was not let off as easily as he thought he would be. His group of close friends, the same people he spent entire evenings hanging out with in the central square of the town, gave him the cold shoulder. They said he couldn't be trusted.

His father had passed away the year before, and none of his five brothers and sisters talked to him now. They said that he was irresponsible; a burden on the family; inconsiderate. That was probably partly true, but he had been that way all of his life. What had suddenly changed? Why did people turn against him, as if he carried some kind of plague?

Everything became clearer when he took someone's advice and went to see Lorenzo. Lorenzo called himself an interpreter, others called him a *shaman*. He was too young to be a shaman, thought Paulo when he first saw him. In his early thirties, with a confident, square jaw and unusually high cheekbones, Lorenzo looked like an ordinary man. The extraordinary thing about him was his occupation – he delivered messages between the worlds, the present reality

– and what he referred to as The Other Side.

Lorenzo would only see someone if he had a message for them. If he didn't, he would send them away.

"I have a message for you," said Lorenzo when Paulo showed up on his doorstep one early evening in June. "My fee is three-hundred kwanza, up front."

Paulo took the crumpled bills out of his pocket, and handed them to Lorenzo. Then he followed him into his small house, breathing in a strange fragrance of sweet grass and bitter herbs.

Lorenzo invited him to sit on a soft, old couch, and went to wash his hands. Then he rubbed them in strange-smelling oil. The smell made Paulo sick, made him feel as if he needed to get out of the room and run away. Still, he didn't move. Lorenzo rubbed the oil on his temples and slowly swayed backwards and forward. He closed his eyes and started talking slowly, as if in his sleep.

"She cursed you," he said.

"Who?" asked Paulo.

"I see an old woman. She has put a powerful curse on you. Only she can remove it."

The thoughts raced in his head. He'd robbed so many people lately, most of them faceless. There were at least two this week, and three or four a week before. These were not violent muggings, he was just seizing opportunities. If people weren't smart enough to look after their things, he would take advantage of it. But a curse? Why?

Then, in a flash, he did recall an old woman. It must have happened a few weeks back, on one of the busier streets. She was walking slowly, leaning on a cane, a bag in her hand. He grabbed the bag and ran. It was easy, but he was disappointed to discover there wasn't anything valuable in the bag. Only three hundred kwanza and some plain black stones. Three hundred kwanza – Lorenzo's fee.

Was this a coincidence? He didn't think much of his find at the time, and threw the empty bag with the stones under a nearby bridge.

"This was your message," said Lorenzo, looking Paulo straight in the eye. He then got up and accompanied him to the door. Paulo hesitated, his face showing the disbelief he struggled with.

"The Other World is real. You have the choice to accept it or to pretend it doesn't exist," said Lorenzo. "I am only an interpreter; I don't decide how things turn out."

That night Paulo thought about Lorenzo's words. The only thing to do, if he believed in this nonsense, would be to try and find the woman and convince her to remove the curse. How he would get her to do it he didn't know, but it seemed a less complex task than actually finding her.

For days Paulo wandered the street where he remembered grabbing the old woman's bag. He spotted many careless strangers, some he took advantage of, others he didn't. But there was no trace of the old woman.

Now she was walking a few steps ahead, vulnerable and frail. He was pretty sure it was her.

He took a few long steps and caught up with her. She seemed unbothered by his presence. She continued walking, completely ignoring the approaching young man.

"*Desculpa,*" he said. "Excuse me, please."

She kept on walking. Paulo quickened his step and stood right in front of her. She stopped.

He looked at her face, and jumped back. Her skin was as wrinkled as a lizard's, but that was not what startled Paulo. It was her eyes, or rather, the lack of them. She had pale blue, large marbles instead of eyeballs, and they stared into the distance, looking through Paulo.

"I can see you," she said. "What do you want?"

Paulo hesitated.

"Speak up, young man," she said.

"Did you put a curse on me?" mumbled Paulo.

"Did you steal my black stones?" asked the woman.

Paulo nodded. She seemed to be satisfied with this reply she couldn't possibly see.

"Then I did curse you," she said.

"Will you remove the curse?" asked Paulo in a small voice.

"Will you give me my stones back?" asked the woman.

Paulo remained silent.

"Go look for my stones, then find me again," said the woman and started walking, pushing Paulo aside with her cane.

"I'll never find them," said Paulo to her back as she walked away.

"Then you will never escape my curse, unless you repent."

The wind carried her words like feathers.

Paulo returned to the bridge where he had thrown the bag weeks ago, but there was no trace of it. Devastated, he went home. Home was now a smelly room in an abandoned house, with no electricity or running water.

The next morning, he returned to the bridge. He scanned the ground carefully and found many round stones, but none of them were black. Then a thought entered his mind – *Will she even see the difference?*

He spent an hour gathering round, smooth stones. He pocketed them and made his way to a construction site he knew of. He dipped the stones in black tar and left them to dry in the hot sun. When they dried, he put them in his pocket and made his way home. Once there, he lay on his thin mattress, turned towards the wall and closed his eyes. His stomach didn't stop hurting all night.

The next morning he returned to where he met the old

woman the previous day. He sat on a broken bench and waited. People walked past, making their belongings an easy target for an opportunist like him. Yet he dared not move. He waited all morning and all afternoon, but the old woman didn't show up. Then he started asking around. The fourth shop owner he talked to recognized her immediately.

"The witch," said the man. "She lives a few streets away. In fact, we deliver some groceries to her every Friday."

"Can I come back on Friday and take the delivery?" asked Paulo.

The shop owner winked. "It'll cost you," he said.

Paulo pulled out the last wrinkled bill from his pocket and handed it to the man.

"Be here at nine," the man said.

Paulo was back on the Friday at nine. He took a grocery bag in each hand, peeking inside to check the content.

He made his way to the old woman's apartment. It was only three blocks away. She lived on the fourth floor, no elevator. He stood for a moment at the bottom of the stairs, trying to work out a plan. His mind went blank.

He then made his way up slowly, stopping at every floor, before he found himself in front of a plain wooden door. It was just like the man at the shop had described to him. He knocked and waited. There was no reply, so he knocked again.

He shuffled from foot to foot and knocked a third time. Still no reply. He put his hand on the handle and pushed it lightly. The door opened without a sound.

He hesitated for a moment, and then stepped inside, finding himself in a narrow, dark corridor. There was a strange odor in the air.

"*Ola*," he said, and waited. There was no answer.

"Hello!" he called again.

Slowly and nervously, he advanced down the corridor. He reached a small room, and looked around him, lowering the bags of groceries to the floor. The front room was dark and empty, except for an old couch and a small table. A large Amazonian wooden mask hung on the wall, its hollow eyes staring at Paulo.

"Hello," he tried again. The silence was as loud as the aftermath of an explosion.

He walked around the apartment, following the strange smell. He found a small kitchen, which looked as if no one had been in it for days. There was a tiny bathroom with a sink and rusty tap. Finally, he saw the bedroom.

In the light that streamed in through the cracks of the shades that were pulled down, he could make out a small figure lying on a large bed. It was the old woman, her eyes closed. She looked as if she was sleeping.

He moved closer to her and slowly raised his arm. He touched her shoulder gently. She opened her eyes, and Paulo jumped back.

"Did you bring me my stones?" she asked.

Paulo felt numb. Slowly, he reached into his pocket and took out a handful of black, smooth stones. Her pale blue eyes looked straight through him. Without a word, he put the stones in her hand. She closed her eyes.

"I am dying," she said.

Paulo remained silent, waiting for his verdict. Would she notice that the stones he gave her were not the ones he had stolen from her?

"Come closer," she whispered.

He sat on the edge of the bed. She held out a frail hand. He took it.

"You will stay here and take care of me until I die," she said. "And then I will forgive you for stealing my stones. And for trying to cheat me on my deathbed."

Paulo gasped.

"Listen carefully," she said.

He listened to her talk in her cracked voice. She gave him detailed instructions on what to do, how to care for her once she died.

"If you do all these things – exactly as I asked you – the curse will be removed, and I will die peacefully," she said.

He sat there for a few moments, speechless. Then he walked out of the room and recovered the shopping bags. He stepped into the small kitchen and took out the groceries. Everything he needed stood before him, on the kitchen counter.

He opened the small, rusty fridge and took out a paper bag. In it were three large, black, shriveled mushrooms. He boiled a pan of water and threw the mushrooms in. Then he waited six minutes, drained the liquid and carefully laid the mushrooms on a piece of paper he found in the second drawer, just as the old woman said he would.

He boiled more water in the same pan, and threw in the ingredients he had just taken out of the shopping bags. He added a few herbs out of a tin he found inside the old, crumbling cupboard. He then added the mushrooms and stirred. Then he inhaled the sickening smell. It made him think of unwashed clothes and mold.

He poured the infusion into a cup and took it to the old woman's deathbed. Kneeling beside her, he helped her sit up. Without thanking him, she took the cup in her shaking hands and sipped the hot liquid with ardor. She leaned back on the pillow and closed her eyes.

Her breath suddenly became steady and calm. Something resembling a smile appeared on her lips. Then she stopped breathing.

Paulo hesitated for a while before he touched her arm. It was still warm, but limp. He studied her features, her wrinkles, her calm expression.

His stomach started turning, and he left the room and sat on the worn sofa. She said to wait for nightfall, so he would.

He kicked his sandals off and put his aching feet up. The old, thin fabric felt cool against them. Paulo surrendered to the weariness that took over him; he fell asleep.

He woke with a start, not remembering where he was. The strange smell still hung like a curtain of thick fog and the air in the room stood still. He got up and tried to open the window. The hinges screeched. Paulo insisted, and the window finally gave.

The fresh night air came rushing in, and he stared at the round moon. It looked to him as if it was mocking him and he felt an urge to howl at it, like a mad dog. His temples pounded, his heart raced. He just couldn't go ahead with it all. He didn't have it in him.

His feet carried him outside the small, stuffy apartment. He ran and ran, pushed ahead by a late-night, strange early-summer wind. He arrived back home just before midnight.

He collapsed on his old, torn mattress. Staring at the shadows that appeared on the dirty wall, he drifted into a dreamless sleep that lasted for hours and hours. It was almost noon when he awoke the next day.

Sitting up in panic, he recalled the previous night's events. Now he was not only a thief, but also a killer. Not only was he cursed; he would be haunted forever if he didn't finish the job. He got up on his feet, realizing with some surprise that he was fully clothed.

He decided to return to the apartment and finish what he should have done the previous night.

He walked out the door and made the forty-minute trip back to the old woman's apartment. He looked at the people walking on the street, the cars driving past him, and saw them in a new light. They looked clearer, brighter. He could not explain this newfound form of vision he was experiencing. His mind was empty.

He finally arrived at the old, crumbling building and ran up the four flights of stairs, taking them two steps at a time. When he reached the familiar door, he pushed the handle without thinking twice.

The door was locked. He tried it again. It wouldn't open. Then he felt something under his shoe, like a lump or a pebble. He lifted his foot and looked at the ground. There he saw six black stones, perfectly round and smooth.

Panic washed over him. He turned and ran down the stairs, down the street, away from the building, as fast as his feet could take him. A paralyzing, icy fear slowly filled his lungs.

Train

The boy looked as if he'd been waiting on the platform for a while – disheveled, his clothes a size too big, his black hair uncombed.

"The train is late, huh?" asked the man who'd just arrived, carrying a battered leather case. The boy just stared ahead.

"A bit rude, young man, not to answer an adult when he's asking you a question," said the man, his hunched shoulders suddenly straightening. The boy shrugged and kicked a small stone down into the rail-pit.

"No luggage, eh? Waiting for someone?" insisted the man.

The boy looked away, towards a few old houses built not far from the tracks. The once-white paint was now a nondescript shade of brown. Even from a distance, it was obvious that the houses were not inhabited – the open doors swinging in the warm afternoon wind, the window frames like hollow eyes, staring onto the rails.

The man gave up and looked for a place to sit. He made his way towards a bench on the far side of the platform, limping slightly. When he reached it, he sat and took a plastic bag out of his battered case. From it, he produced a sandwich.

The boy watched from the corner of his eye as the man slowly unwrapped his sandwich and examined its content. He slowly brought the unwrapped sandwich to his open mouth. Just before his teeth closed on it, he noticed the boy staring. The man put the sandwich down, motioning with it, as if asking – *Would you like some?*

The boy's eyes darted away and focused on the tip of his own shoe.

"Don't be shy, young man, have a bite to eat," called the man. Clumps of his thin hair were blowing in the afternoon wind, exposing a vulnerable scalp.

The boy raised his eyes for a split second and looked down at the tracks, only to look away again.

"Suit yourself," called the man and bit into his sandwich. A drop of tomato juice leaked onto his light spring-jacket, dotting it red. He ate slowly, chewing every bite, curiously examining the boy who continued staring at the rails.

Another passenger arrived, an elderly woman. She dragged a small suitcase, her hair protected from the late-afternoon wind by a green scarf tied under her chin.

She stopped and balanced her suitcase against the wall, then nodded in greeting at the man. He nodded back.

"The train is late?" she asked, and the man jumped to his feet. He shook some crumbs off his trousers, wiped his mouth with the back of his hand, grabbed his case and approached the elderly lady, his limp more pronounced this time.

"Yes, ma'am," he said cheerfully. "Been waiting for nearly thirty minutes."

"Oh, I was worried that I missed it," said the woman in a soft voice.

"No, ma'am, should arrive any moment now. These trains normally run every half-hour."

The lady smiled at him, relieved. Her hand played with the pearl brooch pinned to the lapel of her taupe jacket. He thought that she probably dressed up for the journey, as elderly people often do when travelling.

"I'm not from around here, myself," said the man. "Been looking at a bar for sale here in town. I'm retiring this year and it's time for me to do what I always wanted to do – open up my own bar, serve good beer, have a good chat with my clients."

"Sounds like a wonderful plan," said the woman.

"The wife died six years ago, daughter all grown up and moved to France, so I'm looking to do something new, away from the stress of the city, you see."

She nodded and they both kept quiet for a while.

"The train is late," the lady commented, and sighed deeply. The man scratched his head, looking for something appropriate to say.

"Yorkville seems like a nice little town," he finally said. "Far from the station, though. Took me twenty minutes to walk here, couldn't see any buses or taxis," he added.

"I live close to the station now; wouldn't want to miss the train again," said the lady. "That's my house, right there," she added, and pointed to one of the abandoned-looking homes.

The man shook his head in surprise, then pointed his chin towards the boy.

"Strange young man," he whispered. "No luggage, doesn't say a word. Quite rude, the youth these days."

"Oh, him," she said. "He always comes here. Likes to look at the tracks. His father used to work here, at this station. Horrible way to die, really. Fell right onto the tracks."

"That's terrible," said the man, suddenly feeling guilty for scolding the boy earlier. "What a shame."

"The train is late," said the woman, arranging a few hairs that had escaped from underneath her green scarf. She rubbed her eyes, as if bothered by the warm wind. She sighed again.

"I'll go and check the timetable," said the man, gallantly. "I'll be right back."

He left his case on the platform, right next to the elderly lady, and walked inside the small station. There was no one around, and the ticket booth was shut. In fact, it looked as if it hadn't been open for a long time, thin cobwebs stuck to the edges of the window seal.

He looked around for a timetable, but couldn't see one, so walked towards the exit. Just as he stepped outside, he saw a young man in blue overalls approaching on a bicycle. He was struggling to balance a large bucket and a broom tied to the back of his bicycle.

"Hello there," the man called to him. "The train is late."

"Excuse me?" said the young man, who now reached the entrance and got off his bicycle. He put the bucket down and rubbed his hands together, to dry them from sweat.

"The train is late; do you by any chance know the timetable?"

The man looked at him and blinked twice.

"The train doesn't stop at this station," said the man. "Hasn't for years."

"But, sir, you are surely mistaken. There are two other passengers waiting on the platform!" exclaimed the older man. "We've been waiting for nearly an hour, now."

"Never seen a train stop here, and I've been cleaning here once in a while for two years," said the young man, leaning his bicycle against the wall. "After the accidents, they shut it down. Said it wasn't safe, and there was no money for renovations. But they pay me to clean here, so I come here every couple of months."

"Accidents?" asked the older gentleman. The young man nodded.

"First, the station manager's son chased his ball, then fell onto the tracks and got hit by the approaching train. Died on the spot, poor boy. A week later an old lady who was late for the train tried to get on as it started moving, and got dragged a few hundred yards before they managed to stop the train. It was too late for her. They shut the station down, and diverted the train through Liphook. Not enough people in Yorkville to need a station now, anyway."

The man stared at the cleaner with disbelief.

"I better tell the other passengers on the platform, then. We must find a way to get to Liphook!" he said, and started back into the station. The cleaner followed him, with a bemused look on his face. The two men walked through the empty station, past the closed ticket window and towards the platform.

"I see no one, sir," said the cleaning man, suddenly distancing himself from the older gentleman. "Is that your case, there, on the platform?"

The elderly man stopped and looked around him in wonder.

"That's impossible," he said. "They were just here, both of them."

He looked around again, but the only thing he could see on the platform was his battered case, and dust flying around in the warm wind.

"I'm afraid there's no public transport from here to Liphook," said the younger man. "It's a twenty-minute walk back to Yorkville and then a bus to the Liphook station."

The older man stood on the platform for a few moments, the warm wind playing with his thin hair, blowing it from side to side. He stared at a green kerchief, fluttering in the wind on the far end of the tracks.

Recognition

"The act of recognizing or condition of being recognized;
An awareness that something perceived has been perceived
before"

The first time she saw him was right after the birth of her second daughter, Abigail. At night, when her newborn daughter was tucked up beside her in a little cot, a boy came in. It was quite late at night, long after visiting hours were over.

He just stood and stared, his hands in the pockets of his jeans. His hair was in a mess and his full bottom lip turned down, sulking. He had a sad, longing look in his eyes.

Anne sat up in her narrow hospital bed, pulling the sheet over her naked shoulders.

"What's your name?" she asked.

He didn't answer. He just looked deep into her large, brown eyes. Then he turned and left the room, quietly closing the door behind him.

He must be the son of one of the nurses, thought Anne. Maybe she had had to bring him along on her night shift.

The next afternoon her husband came to pick her up. They took their bundle of joy home, wrapped up in a soft welcoming blanket. Abigail was well-protected against the February frost.

Her older daughter, Emma, had just turned four. Anne was a little worried about her daughter's reaction, of the jealousy she might feel towards this little intruder her mom had just brought home from the hospital.

Emma was a smart little girl. She loved drawing and adored music. She didn't have too many friends, but most of the books Anne consulted assured that it was quite normal for Emma's age. *She is the quiet type,* thought Anne.

Now that her little sister was home, at first Emma seemed to withdraw even more. But after a couple of mild jealous attacks, demanding her mom's attention when she was bathing or dressing the baby, she adjusted quite well to the new reality. She helped with her little sister, Abigail, whenever she was asked. She brought clean diapers when she needed changing. She handed her toys, sang and told her stories.

The only thing that now worried Anne was that Emma started talking about this friend of hers, Elliot. There was nothing wrong with having a new friend. In fact, under normal circumstances, it would have made Anne quite happy. Except, this friend was imaginary.

Emma said he lived in the closet in her room, and came out to play only when her mom was not there.

"He is very shy," she said. "He thinks you don't want him around, so he hides from you."

"It is a way for her to cope with the new situation," said Emma's teacher. "Children at this age often have imaginary friends. It helps them cope with stress and with changing reality."

"She'll be fine," said Anne's husband, David. "I had an imaginary friend when I was her age. He was a dragon."

Anne even asked Abigail's pediatrician about Emma's imaginary friend.

"Imaginary friends are an important form of companionship for children," the pediatrician said. "It does not signify a problem or disorder, unless it begins to interfere with everyday social interactions," she added knowingly.

So Anne took this worry off her mind, and concentrated on caring for her two daughters. She tried to spend as much time as possible with Emma, to give her as much attention as she could.

Then she saw him again. It was about three weeks after Abigail was born. Emma was at day-care, and she was pushing Abigail's stroller in the park. It was a sunny but cold day in late March, and the baby was well wrapped up, her little face almost invisible in a thick pink hat.

Anne sat on the bench, looking at the older children playing in the park. Then she saw him.

He was wearing a thin shirt. Again, he had his hands deep in the pockets of his jeans.

He seemed to be eight or nine years old. His pale face was surrounded by sand-washed hair. He had a rejected, upset air about him.

Anne recognized him immediately. It was the boy from the maternity. She waved.

He didn't wave back. He just stood there and looked at her with sad longing in his watery, wide brown eyes.

He stared at her for three or four minutes before Anne got up and walked towards him. She wanted to talk to him, to ask why he wasn't playing with the others; why wasn't he wearing a coat on this cold day.

When she was only a few steps away, Abigail started crying. Anne stopped to smile and touch her daughter's gloved hand.

"It's okay, sweetie," she said and lightly rocked the stroller. When she looked up, the boy was gone.

She only started feeling uncomfortable when she saw him for the third time, a couple of weeks later. This time he was standing on her front lawn.

She was reading a book while Abigail was taking a nap. She raised her eyes from the page and looked outside for a moment.

There he was, standing in the same proud, lonely manner, with his hands in his pockets. The look in his eyes pained her. It was a look of loneliness, of deep sorrow. She felt bad for him.

She got up to open the door. She wanted to invite him in for a hot chocolate, although she thought it was strange that he was standing outside her house. Maybe he followed her home, she said to herself.

By the time she opened the door, he was gone.

"I think I am going mad," she complained that afternoon to her best friend, Rebecca. "I keep seeing this boy everywhere, and when I try to talk to him – he vanishes."

Rebecca shook her curly head.

"You just had a baby, and you're not getting enough sleep," she said.

Anne hesitated. "It is just that… I should have had a boy his age," she whispered. Her eyes filled with tears.

"It was about ten years ago, and I was with this guy, Thomas. I got pregnant – didn't really mean to, but it happened. I only realized I was pregnant when I was four months into it – so I went about my life as usual at first. Didn't really take care of myself. I always wondered what would have happened if I had been more careful – partied less, drank less," said Anne in a quiet voice.

Rebecca patted her friend's arm. "So what happened?" she asked.

"He was a very small baby, didn't develop very well, and…and he died two days after he was born. Everyone said it was not my fault, but I always felt a little guilty. Then Thomas and I broke up, which was a way to get away from the whole awful experience. But maybe if I took better care back then, if I wanted this baby more, really wanted him, then…"

"Now you have two wonderful daughters and a great husband," said Rebecca. "Don't feel bad about what happened ten years ago."

Anne nodded and wiped the tears that rolled down her cheek.

"I still think about it sometimes," she said.

That evening Anne couldn't stop thinking about the boy, wondering who he was. He looked so lonely, so longing to be loved.

He must have run away from home, she decided. *For some strange reason, he is following me. He does look like he needs a good bath and some loving attention.*

Then she pushed the upsetting thoughts out of her mind.

The following week, on a rainy afternoon, she sat on the floor with Emma, doing a puzzle. Abigail was gurgling beside them in her crib.

The music from the animal mobile over Abigail's crib made Anne sleepy. It didn't seem to have the same effect on Abigail. She was kicking her little legs in the air.

The puzzle had one-hundred pieces and took a lot of concentration. It wasn't easy to put together, but Emma shuffled the pieces around on the floor with her usual patience, until she found the one she was looking for.

Anne counted her blessings; two healthy, gorgeous girls. So what if she was so tired she couldn't keep her eyes open? She would sleep early tonight.

Then she raised her head. Her eyes fell on the boy, wearing his same jeans and thin shirt. This time he was sitting on the armchair, only a few steps away from them. His face was even paler than she remembered. Something about him didn't look right, didn't look real.

Anne screamed and grabbed Emma. Then she started for the crib.

"Who are you? How did you get in here?" she cried, feeling her throat blocking with fear.

He didn't answer. He wiped his cheek with the back of his dirty palm and shrugged.

Anne felt her daughter's little hand stroking her cheek. She looked at her and saw her calm, smiling face.

"It's okay, Mom," said Emma, reaching for the piece of the puzzle she dropped when her mother grabbed her a minute before. "This is Elliot."

Anne looked at Elliot. He was still there, but his face got paler and paler. He looked very worried.

"He wants to live here with us, Mom," said Emma. "He doesn't know anyone else. He says he is lonely."

Anne felt paralyzed; she looked down at her daughter's hopeful face.

"Can he please, please, live with us, Mom?" Emma asked. "He says he is my brother."

The Café

I hadn't seen my grandparents in over ten years. As a child, I spent many pleasant afternoons and weekends in their small apartment, which always smelled of my grandmother's baking and my grandfather's Old English cologne.

My parents were young, hard-working and ambitious, and they counted on Grandma Ana and Grandpa Jacob to help look after their only granddaughter.

They hadn't changed; they looked just as I remembered. Grandpa Jacob held his arms out and I rushed to embrace him. He kissed me on both cheeks. His kisses were wet, and as a child I often squirmed away from them, but this time I didn't.

He was still using his Old English cologne. The smell tickled my nostrils. I sneezed, and rushed to embrace Grandma Ana. We didn't know what to say. It'd been so long.

We sat down at a small table at the café they'd suggested, little lanterns on every table, giving the impression of being in the dining room of a cruise-ship or in the restaurant wagon of a train. The background music was mellow and the waiters glided around quietly, serving a handful of other customers who whispered to each other, afraid to disturb the silence and the misty ambience.

"So, how have you been?" asked Grandma Ana. Her green eyes sparkled behind her reading glasses, the same ones I used to try on in front of her mirror fifteen years back.

"I'm good, really good," I said. "Lots of things have happened since the last time we met."

"We know," said my grandfather, smiling proudly. "We've been following your progress."

"Would you like to order?" asked a waiter dressed in a white shirt and black waistcoat and trousers. He handed us three menus and floated away.

"What would you like? The chicken with potatoes or the beef with rice?" asked my grandmother, just like she used to do when I was ten or twelve years old.

"I would like an aperitif, if that's ok," I said. "Maybe a glass of white wine?"

"Good idea," said Grandpa Jacob. "Let's have a bottle."

He ordered a bottle of Chardonnay and some nibbles – olives, small squares of feta cheese, a plate of fresh cut vegetables and a dip.

I studied the menu and noticed a particularity about it.

"Please limit your stay to two hours," it said on the back of the menu. "Those who overstay will not be welcomed back."

How strange, I thought, but didn't mention it to them. After all, they had suggested this place, and anyway, Grandma Ana started telling me about her sister Ella and what news she'd had from her over the past ten years. Ella always loved cats; now she had lots of them, said Grandma Ana.

It was wonderful to listen to my grandmother talk, and it suddenly felt as if the ten years had vanished and we were all just like we were when I was a girl and they were my favorite, loving grandparents.

I had a son of my own now, but Grandpa Jacob and Grandma Ana had never met him.

They wanted to hear all about him, about me, about my

husband, about my life.

"We already know most of these things," said Grandma, "but it's wonderful to hear it from you."

After our wine and snacks we ordered the meal, which was quite tasty. Grandpa ordered a chicken dish and Grandma ordered fish. I went for the beef with rice.

I told Grandma that what I really wanted was a taste of her cooking, the clear chicken soup with bits of carrot that were crunchy and salty, those delicious sweet cheese balls with *crème fraiche* she used to make for my dessert.

"You remember," she said happily.

"Of course I remember, I've been dreaming about your cheese balls for years!" I exclaimed. She smiled contentedly.

We talked and talked, and I noticed that it was now past midnight. We'd surely stayed over two hours, but who cared? It'd been years since I'd seen them, and we had so much to talk about.

"We should probably go," said Grandma Ana. "It's getting late for you."

"I'll pay for the meal," I said. They didn't object, so I stood up and walked towards the bar, to take care of the bill.

"Can I pay, please?" I asked the gentleman behind the cash-register. He flipped through a little receipt book and identified the right one. He then looked at his watch.

"You overstayed," he said gloomily.

"You can't be serious," I said. "I haven't seen my grandparents for years. If you are so strict about this time-limitation, next time I'll take them to another restaurant."

The man looked me straight in the eye and didn't say a word. He handed me the bill, which I paid silently. His dark eyes followed my hand as I collected the change and put it in my pocket. I dropped a few coins in the tips jar on the bar.

"Thank you," I said, "and goodnight."

He nodded and turned away.

I returned to the table and helped my grandmother put on her coat. My grandfather hugged me and wanted to kiss me again. I allowed him.

We stepped towards the exit, and got ready to leave.

"When will I see you again?" I asked them.

They shook their head and pointed at a small sign by the restaurant door. It said exactly the same thing as the menu – meals were limited to two hours and those who overstayed would not be welcomed back.

"I'm afraid we won't be allowed to return here," said my grandfather in a sad voice.

"So we'll meet somewhere else!" I exclaimed. "This time-restriction is totally unreasonable, and there are plenty of other good restaurants."

My grandmother shook her head. She then took my hand and together we stepped back, to look at the neon sign above the restaurant's door. It said "Café of the Deceased".

I wanted to protest, to ask why they didn't warn me, but then I woke up with a start. The fragrant scents of Old English cologne and warm, sweet cheese balls still lingered in my nostrils.

Clockworks

It was a stunning watch. I bought it with my last United Nations salary, when my contract came to an end and I decided to go back to my native Toronto.

"You are too efficient to be working at the UN," said Ursula, soon to become my ex-colleague, as we shared one last meal in the *Palais des Nations* cafeteria. We had shared numerous long lunches there during the five years that my 'career' at the UN had lasted.

"I had all these ideas of changes to be made, improvements to be had. What can I say? It just got too much for my boss," I had replied, and it is true that when I was politely told by the lady in HR that my contract would not be renewed, I actually sighed in relief.

So I went out and bought this watch, a souvenir from my time in Geneva, which, all things taken into account, had been great fun. I'd made many friends here, and lived in a small apartment in the Pâquis. I'd had a nice, padded paycheck. A fair amount of dates. What else could an average thirty-something-year-old want?

I am a former journalist, and I guess I missed the adrenaline rush a good story gives. There had been none of that at the UN. So when I returned to Canada I got my old job back at a small local paper, the *Toronto Gazette*. If I agreed to write the social column, it was only because I knew there were better things to come.

That's when I noticed it. I first became suspicious when I missed the seven o'clock news by a couple of minutes.

Was my fabulous Swiss watch wrong?

It was a beautiful time-telling instrument, titanium and gold-leaf combined to perfection in a work of art that took my breath away every time I glanced at my wrist. An upper-end Swiss watch, which was supposed to be as accurate as the measures of salt in a chef's signature dish. Or at least it was, when I bought it back in Geneva.

Now, in Toronto, I've had to adjust the time twice a week. It was losing a few minutes every day! How could this be?

Then I went back to Geneva for my winter break, to see old friends and get some good skiing with Vanessa, this beautiful woman I was now dating. She was adequately impressed when I took her to a chalet in Verbier and there, by the blazing fire, we spent ten evenings of sizzling passion drenched in mulled wine and very occasional fondue outings with old friends.

I was so taken by Vanessa and her deep hazel eyes, that I nearly forgot the main thing I wanted to do on my way to the airport in Geneva – stop by that shop where I bought my watch, to see what could be done about the problem I was experiencing. Surely a Swiss watchmaker would take pride in his profession and understand my dissatisfaction.

The shop attendant looked at my watch, which I'd bought less than a year before.

"It's a beautiful piece," he said. "Very well-made."

"But it isn't accurate," I complained. "It loses several minutes every week. Who wants an inaccurate Swiss watch?"

The man looked at me with surprise.

"This watch has a mechanical mechanism, sir," he said, looking at me through his narrow, rectangular spectacles. "It is not as accurate as cheap, quartz mechanisms. A sophisticated gentleman like yourself surely knows that".

The stern-looking gentleman turned my watch back and forth in his palm, and watched it run the course of a minute, its perfect long hand delicately bouncing from twelve, back to twelve again. He then examined the proof of purchase and guarantee which I'd produced from my wallet, and glanced at my suitcase and at the beautiful girl waiting for me, nervously checking her own watch.

"I see you are on your way to the airport, sir," he said politely. "If you'd like, I will exchange this watch for you for another, with a quartz mechanism. Perhaps it will better suit your needs."

I hesitated, but Vanessa was making anxious signs at me. We would miss our flight if we didn't hurry.

"Although your watch looks fine to me, it is still under guarantee, and we like our customers to be satisfied with their purchases. We take pride in our watches," said the man, still holding my watch in his palm.

I thanked him as I left his shop, wearing the new watch on my wrist – a different model of the same make, still beautifully crafted, but with a quartz mechanism. This should solve the accuracy problem, I was told.

We made the flight on time, and slept through most of the ten-hour journey back to Canada. It saddened me to part with Switzerland and with all the friends I'd revisited, but somehow I knew I would be back.

The Canadian winter was cold and bitter that year, and the break-up with Vanessa didn't help. After our wonderful escape to Switzerland, she'd decided that I wasn't such a hot catch after all, and started dating some big-shot lawyer who drove a Lexus and took her out every night to expensive restaurants.

The grief over the short, depressing days and the collapse of my love affair was compounded by the discovery that my watch was losing time again.

One Saturday afternoon, I sat in my rented apartment on Bay Street and stared at my computer screen. I had a clock running on the screen, set at GMT, and watched the long hand tick for over an hour. My mind empty of thoughts, I just let it drift, until I glanced down at my own watch, and compared its hand to the one on the screen in front of me. Then I counted, and counted again, and again – and again!

Was it losing one second each and every hour? I took a pen and paper, and calculated that would make twenty-four seconds a day, nearly three minutes a week, and twelve minutes a month…. How was this possible?

"You're losing it, Josh," said my friend Daniel who stopped for a beer later that evening, as he walked out the door on his way to a date with this chick he met the week before at a party. "You need a new girlfriend."

I shrugged it off, and spent the entire evening in front of the computer screen, watching the time tick on. With Pink Floyd in the background, I surrendered to the pleasant melancholy that 'Comfortably Numb' always wrapped me in. And I counted carefully.

By the early hours of the morning I had my proof! My watch was definitely losing a second every hour.

On Sunday I went to my parents' house for lunch. They glanced at each other with worry when I told them how I'd spent the previous evening, and in fact, most of the night.

"Is everything all right? Anything you want to talk about?" asked my dad as he poured some more apple juice into my glass. He thought I wouldn't notice that he pushed the bottle of wine further away from me.

Then I went home and wrote an elaborate letter of complaint to the watch company, with copies to the Geneva Chamber of Commerce, the *Geneva Times* and the Federation of the Swiss Watch Industry. This time they wouldn't be able to blame the mechanical mechanism. And they should know what their watchmakers were up to, ruining the reputation of the entire Swiss watch industry. I described my dissatisfaction with purchasing a watch worth some people's monthly salary, only to find out that it was also costing me three minutes a week! What a waste of time!

A couple of months passed, as I went about with my daily life. I took off my wristwatch and carefully placed it in its original case, in my bedside drawer. It annoyed me too much to even look at it. I replaced it with a cheap Casio, which I didn't have to take off in the shower, and which better suited my renewed position as a small-time journalist earning a meager weekly paycheck.

And then the letter arrived. It was not only a letter – it was accompanied by a business-class ticket to Switzerland! I couldn't believe my eyes.

"Dear Sir," the letter said. "We deeply apologize for the inconvenience you've experienced and for your dissatis-faction with our product. To make up for this unpleasant experience, we would like to offer you a business-class ticket and a week's stay at a five-star hotel, courtesy of our company. You will be met at the airport by a chauffeured limousine, which will then take you to a meeting at our offices. Please accept our sincere apologies. We look forward to welcoming you to Switzerland, the world center of watches."

The letter was signed by Mr. Jean-Pierre LeMontre, the president of the company, and it left me speechless. I looked at the date on the ticket – only a week away. What could I say? Of course I asked my boss for a week off work – I didn't have any other summer holiday planned – and got on that Swissair flight to Geneva, through Zurich.

As promised, the chauffeur awaited me, carrying a small sign with my name printed on it. It was late June, the end of a glorious Geneva summer day, the clean streets glimmering in the setting sun. Despite my tiredness and the late hour, the chauffeur insisted on taking me straight to that meeting with the representative of the company.

"Can't it wait until tomorrow?" I asked hopefully. I could only imagine myself walking the cobbled streets of the old town again, sipping a cold beer in one of the bars.

"I am afraid not, sir," my chauffeur said gravely. "I was instructed to take you straight to our offices. They are expecting you."

What else could I do? I let him take my small case and put it in the trunk of his fancy car, and then I sunk back into the leather seat, staring at the highway flying past me. To my surprise, the car headed toward the border, and crossed into neighboring France – a daily affair for many who live in one country and take the twenty-minute journey to the other, at the end of each working day.

"Where are we going?" I leaned forward and asked my mustached chauffeur.

"We are nearly there, sir," was all he offered in return.

The car went past Ferney Voltaire and past the small villages of Ornex and Sègny, each home to only several hundred people or so. When it turned right towards Cessy, I was really puzzled. What watch company was there in the small, remote village of Cessy?

We pulled to a halt in front of a plain, square building. I recognized it immediately. It was part of the CERN network, the European Organization for Nuclear Research, which was running a Minotaur's Labyrinth under most of the French villages neighboring Geneva.

Baffled, I stepped out of the car and let the chauffeur escort me into the building – which inside looked more like an airplane hangar than an office building. We took a small elevator that went down, deeper and deeper into the ground. I realized that my hands were sweating.

"Where are we going?" I now demanded in a voice that wasn't my own.

"Nearly there, sir," came the swift reply. The uniformed man looked straight ahead, avoiding my eyes.

As the elevator door opened, two men in overalls waited for us, and escorted me into a small office where a white-haired man sat behind a large desk. He got to his feet to greet me.

"Mr. Pickering, welcome to CERN," he said as he offered a firm handshake.

"What the hell…?" I started.

"Please sit down," he asked quietly and I heard the door close behind me. It was just him and me in that room, over 300 feet underground.

I nervously sat on the simple wooden chair, suddenly feeling the tiredness of the long journey and the stiffness of my shoulders. I waited for him to speak.

"We seem to have a bit of a situation here, Joshua," said the man in front of me. "May I call you Joshua?"

All I could do was stare at him and nod. He smiled a thin smile.

"Apparently you've expressed some concerns, and you've expressed them extensively. Your concerns are regarding time, I was told. Apparently you bought a Swiss watch and noticed that it was built according to Swiss time, which seems to pass slightly slower than the time in your own country. "

The realization of what the man in front of me was about to say began to sink in. I nodded silently.

"We've researched your background, Joshua Pickering. You are a clever man. So I will confide in you, and tell you that there are some unexpected effects of the recent CERN Big Bang experiment. Nothing like the black holes that the newspapers were writing about. All that was just journalistic hype that has nothing to do with reality. But we are experiencing a minor loss of time. Just a second every hour, twenty-four seconds every day. You'll be glad to know that this is only in the time zone which CERN is in."

"But...I was in Canada...why did it happen there?" the words slipped out of my mouth before I was able to stop them.

"Unfortunately, it now seems to have affected the Swiss watch industry, as they are constructing their watches according to Swiss time." A sarcastic smile appeared on the man's face. "Swiss time appears to be less accurate than it was a year or two ago," he added. "No one really noticed this so far. But you have."

I nodded, speechless. What was he going to do next? Have me shot and bury my body in this nuclear research facility? Use it as fuel for their famous particles accelerator?

He slowly opened a drawer in his desk, and I felt myself beginning to shake. Would he pull out a gun?

Instead, he pulled out a sheet of paper, and laid it in front of me. I stared at it.

"Mr. Pickering. Joshua. I would like to offer you a job with us, as a media-liaison for the team investigating this time lapse we've been experiencing. This is on the condition that you will respect our code of confidentiality, of course. This is a matter that is better kept quiet for now, although I am sure we will have to give some explanations in due course. However, we do need to work these explanations out first."

Suddenly I could breathe again. I looked down at the contract before me. It offered even better conditions than I had at the UN. I looked up at the man in front of me, my future boss, and hesitated only for a few seconds. Then I initialed every page, and signed at the bottom.

Gemmi Travelers

"It's a very old mountain pass," said Gregory, pointing to the map in front of them. "It connects the Swiss cantons of Valais and Bern. Here's the Daubenhorn in the west, almost ten thousand feet, and the Plattenhornern, nearly as high, to the east. It cannot be travelled by road, but it is directly accessible by cable car from Leukerbad."

Laurent was not very interested in history, or geography. He liked nature, and more than anything, he liked taking photographs. He intended to take as many as he could while vacationing in Switzerland.

"Are you going to haul this huge camera bag up into the mountains? What about your tent?" asked Gregory.

"I'll be fine in my thick sleeping bag," said Laurent to the group of young men that he had met a day earlier at the hostel in Leukerbad. When he'd heard that they were going to hike and spend the night at a refuge in the mountains, he asked if he could join them, and they agreed.

"Doesn't sound like a good idea to me," said Gregory. "You never know when you might need a tent, the refuge is sometimes full. But do as you wish. Just don't expect me to carry you down if you freeze to death up there."

"I won't," said Laurent as he carefully arranged the huge lenses in his pack. "No point in taking this trip, if I can't get some good pictures. And I can't carry both things, so I'll have to give the tent a miss."

"Right," said Gregory, who was the most experienced hiker in the group – a Swiss-born American, who'd been hiking in the Alps since he was a boy.

They left Leukerbad early in the morning, a pale sun rising behind them, their backpacks loaded with supplies, sleeping bags and tents. Laurent stared at the Gemmiwand rock-face before him; his heavy walking boots crushing the crisp crust of ice formed on the ground on this frosty morning in early May, as if it were a thin potato chip. The short walk from their hostel, where they left the rest of their belongings in storage for a couple of days, to the bottom of the cable car, took only ten minutes. Patches of snow on the peaks around them shimmered in the sun like icing on a cake. A few more weeks and most of these would be gone, melted by the warm spring sun.

The cable car, designed to carry thirty people, was mostly empty. The handful of others who were in with them this early mid-week morning were tourists planning a short walk by the half-frozen lake at the top.

The ride up took only a few minutes, and Laurent could hardly contain his excitement. They all stared at the approaching cliff-face as the wind rocked the heavy metal cradle.

The cabin finally reached the top and clicked onto its rails. The doors opened; the few passengers walked out, as if into a land of fantasy. Lake Daubensee stretched below them to the end of the valley, blue as the skies on this crisp spring morning, and they started walking towards it.

They marched in silence for two hours, before Gregory suggested they stop to sip some hot, sweet tea from his large thermos. Laurent was glad that Greg suggested the stop – he wouldn't have dared to suggest one himself.

They drank the hot liquid with gratitude. Then they continued for another hour or two, before stopping for a late lunch. It was after six when Laurent felt he could go no farther. The sun would set in an hour or so and the lighting was perfect for that series of shots he'd been dreaming about for weeks.

"We have another half hour of walking before we get to the refuge," said Greg. "Whoever gets there first, gets priority. There are only ten beds available and I don't feel like camping outside tonight."

"I'll join you there," said Laurent. "I have to stop for some pictures, right here."

"Bad idea," said Greg. "You'll end up sleeping outside if you don't hurry. They won't let us save you a bed if other hikers arrive there before you."

"I've got to take these pictures now, the lighting is perfect," said Laurent. "I'll be fine."

Greg shrugged.

"I suppose you can always borrow my tent and sleep outside," he said and showed Laurent the location of the refuge on his map.

The group continued, and Laurent lowered his heavy pack and pulled out the camera and tripod. He set it up and stood, motionless, stunned by the beauty surrounding him. He was transfixed by the mixture of primary colors blending into something that the naked eye could not capture and define, but the camera certainly could.

He waited for the sun to touch the peak before him and took a series of shots he was certain would make one of his best. By the time he had unscrewed and cleaned his lenses of the dust that had started blowing around him, and packed his camera and tripod, the sun had set.

He started walking. There was nothing around him but rocks and shrubbery; small patches of ice, now invisible in the dark, made him slip, and he scraped his palms. He was careful that his camera did not get damaged.

It was after nine when he admitted to himself that he was lost. The moon over his head was too thin to light the way; a nasty wind had picked up. Had he had a tent he would have stopped and set it up, but of course, he didn't. He started cursing his bad luck; then his own stupidity.

Suddenly he got a whiff of something – some sort of animal smell. What animal would be wandering around at night on this mountain? Surely no more than a chamois. But then he thought he heard voices and started walking towards them. The next thing he noticed was a flickering light.

"Hey," he called. "Hey guys!"

He quickened his step, encouraged by the signs of people nearby. Perhaps he'd not been lost, after all, merely a bit disoriented.

He approached the voices and the lights, and nearly bumped into two mules tied to a rock. It clearly wasn't his own group, but at least he wouldn't be alone. He walked past the mules and was puzzled to see a group of men – ten, maybe twelve, dressed in close-fitting doublets and long boots. They were wrapped in warm furs, sitting around a fire, speaking in hushed voices. They stopped talking when they heard him approach.

He stared at them, and they stared back at him and at his high-tech walking boots and backpack. They examined him as if he was an alien life-form.

"*Vo wo sind Sie cho, Fremde? Vo Curmilz?*" asked one of them, in a guttural language – it sounded like German to him, but he wasn't sure.

"I am sorry," he said. "I...I am lost. And I don't speak German."

The men just stared at him, motionless.

"*Français, peut-être?*" tried Laurent. His French was limited, but he was hoping it was good enough to communicate his need of assistance.

The face of a big, bearded man lit up.

"*Ah, français,*" he said, waving his hands, and continued with a series of sentences in some kind of strange French-like language that Laurent could not comprehend. He prided himself on speaking some French, but this was…something very different.

The men invited him to join them, he could figure that much from their body language. They offered him dried meat and wine, and he thanked them, in English and in French. They just nodded. As he pulled the sleeping bag out from the bottom of his pack and rolled it out by the fire, one of the men said something. The others laughed. He couldn't understand the joke, but he was too tired to care. As long as they let him sleep amongst them, by their fire, he would be all right.

The night got colder. He slipped inside his sleeping bag and closed his eyes. Their voices started fading away. Someone repeated a word: *Curmilz, Curmilz.* He fell asleep.

The next morning he awoke at the crack of dawn. He was alone under the dim, grey skies. Confused, he looked around. No sign of the men, the fire, the camp. He rubbed his eyes, took out the remains of the bottled water he had tucked away in his pack and started heading back towards the Gemmi Pass.

In daylight, with a map at hand, he felt much better. In a few hours he would be found, or find his own way back. He couldn't be lost for long here – many hikers passed this area during the day. Including that strange group of men, he thought and smiled. Perhaps they were part of some local sect?

He walked for three or four hours before he saw the first hiker, and asked for directions. Much as he thought, the Gemmi Pass was not far ahead, and he thanked the fellow traveler. Encouraged, he drank the last sip of his water.

He felt a sense of achievement, as he took some wonderful pictures the day before and made it through the night on the mountain, but then it hit him: he should have taken some pictures of those men. That would have been something.

He was relieved to have made it down to the cable car, and even more relieved to see Gregory and the others waiting there.

"Man, we were just about to alert the police," said Greg, clearly annoyed. They had cut their hike short in order to go and look for him. Now they would all go back to Leukerbad, to their hostel and to the thermal baths, and wash off this whole experience.

"I am sorry," said Laurent to the group. "I really am."

Most of the young men just nodded at him silently. They were clearly not impressed with his inconsiderate behavior.

"So what happened?" asked Gregory on their way down in the cable car. The others simply ignored Laurent.

Laurent told him about his nocturnal encounter. Gregory shook his head disbelievingly.

"You're hallucinating!" he said, and the others, who had been listening to the conversation, laughed.

The cable car operator, an old man in his mid-seventies, looked at the group with clear, blue eyes. He didn't say a word, until they made it back down to Leukerbad, and the other passengers had left the cable car.

He then touched Laurent's shoulder as he walked out of the metal carriage.

"Don't listen to your friends, son. What you said, was that true?" he asked in heavily German-accented English.

"Yes, it was."

"Then you, like a few others in trouble on this mountain, have enjoyed their hospitality. You are a very lucky man, son."

"They? Who are they?"

"The ancient travelers, son. The travelers of Curmilz. They were the bearers, the porters who walked this path some four hundred years back. Some say they still cross the bridge between the two cantons, their ancestral land."

"Curmilz... yes, they said that. What does it mean?"

"It is the old name for the Gemmi Pass, son. It means passage, or peak. Many years ago this passage was only used by bearers, porters. But nowadays, nowadays..." The old man sighed.

"Are you coming, Laurent?" called Gregory impatiently. "We're going back to the hostel. And then I will no longer feel responsible for you."

The old man waved at Laurent. He waved back, and started walking towards town, his heavy boots pacing on the paved road, his eyes glancing up to the Gemmi Pass, the ancient bridge route.

The Right Place

She caught a glimpse of him as she stopped at the gas station on the other side of town. This was getting creepy.

When she drove past him the fourth time that week she began to think – *This is weird. How likely is it that in such a large town I'll cross paths with the same stranger on a regular basis, until he no longer feels like an unknown?*

She was pretty sure he was new in town, probably moved somewhere in the neighborhood – because she saw him shopping once at the local Trader Joe's.

It was the unsettling feeling the sight of him steered inside her that was the most bizarre. It was as if she knew him from somewhere, as if she ought to remember who he was, and had just forgotten. It was a sensation of unsettling familiarity. But as hard as she thought about it, she could not recall a past encounter with this man. He must have been in his mid-to-late forties – so at least a decade older than her. Where did she know him from?

Sarah decided to say something next time she saw him, but their paths did not seem to cross in such a way that they could actually speak. It was more like two trains passing at the station, moving parallel to one another, but not on the same tracks.

"How romantic," said her friend Natalie when she tried to tell her of the weird coincidence. "Is he good-looking?"

"It's not about that," said Sarah. "It's just the strangeness of crossing paths with someone suddenly, again and again, as if there is some kind of point to it, some sort of interaction waiting to happen."

"Interaction, huh?" said Natalie with a smirk, and Sarah decided to drop it. What was the point? She could not put this strange feeling into words, and Natalie would only make fun of it all.

Then she recognized his thin frame and mop of dark hair as she entered Trader Joe's one Saturday morning. She noticed he wore glasses that made him look somewhat bookish. *Maybe he's the intellectual type,* she thought to herself. She took a deep breath, and said hello.

"Hi," he replied and hurried towards the fruit section, busying himself with choosing some green apples. That was when she noticed he was limping, slightly dragging his right foot behind him. It made him endearing to her, as if he was a wounded puppy or a bird with a broken wing. She wondered what had happened to him. But then he disappeared, perhaps to the other side of the store, perhaps onto the street, without as much as giving her another glance.

So much for an attempt at a conversation, she thought. He seemed to have absolutely no interest in her, and she wasn't even sure that she had any interest in him, and if she did – then why. He was not good-looking, not in the immediate, masculine, pick-me-up kind of way. But there was something else about him, something that made her curious.

Deep in her thoughts, she left the store with a shopping bag in her hand. It was the screeching of brakes that shook her out of her daydream, but it was the weight of the man on top of her that prevented the car from hitting her as she started crossing the parking lot, absent-minded.

"Look where you're going, lady!" shouted the driver and added a curse word or two. He drove off, muttering under his breath.

The man got off her and helped her up.

"That was stupid of me. I really wasn't looking where I was going," she said.

He nodded. "I noticed," he said.

"How can I thank you?" she asked.

From up-close she noticed his deep hazel eyes behind the glasses, his high cheekbones.

He examined her with those brown eyes and shook his head.

"No need to thank me, but do watch where you're going. That's the biggest service you can do for me."

She was surprised by his answer, but couldn't think of anything else to say as he made a small parting gesture and walked away.

She went about her daily life, from her day-job designing magazine ads for small businesses to her favorite moments of the week: contemporary dance classes which made her feel as if she could fly, if she wanted to, during the hour and thirty minutes that the classes lasted. *If I lived again,* she thought, *I would become a dancer.* But where she came from, you had to study a profession first, then make time for hobbies. So she studied design, and earned a decent living. *But there must be more to life than this,* she thought. More than occasional dinners with friends, and even more occasional dates with men she had nothing in common with.

Then, on a night when the moon was as round and yellow as a polished gold coin, Sarah walked back from her dance class towards her apartment block on a back street, and something just wasn't right. She got this feeling inside her, an unexplainable fear of the night, of the dark alley she was crossing, of the sound of her own heels against the dusty sidewalk. She felt unsettled that day, and probably the day before that, too, but she tried to shrug it off.

"Don't be such a wimp," she said to herself out loud.

When she felt the rough hand against her mouth, preventing her from screaming, preventing her from breathing, it felt familiar. The hand she always knew would come one day, suddenly, unexpectedly, trying to take away her trust in people, in the good of the world.

She tried to scream but all that came out was a muffled 'ah' before whoever was holding her started dragging her backwards, behind a large container at the corner of the alley and the dark street, away from the comforting moonlight.

What stunned her most was the pace it all took place – so fast she could not grasp the sequence of events, yet it was so slow that she could recall every little detail with every one of her senses – the smell, the touch, the sound of it. Even the bitter taste of the dirty fingers pressing against her mouth. It was her sense of sight she didn't want to use, for fear of seeing who it was that was capable of such a beastly act, of dragging a young woman who had never done anything wrong to him – or to anyone else as far as she could recall – into a dark alley. She tried to stop herself from thinking 'no, no' and 'why, why' and she felt her body become as limp as a rag in the arms that were pulling her under a blanket of fog. The last thing she heard before she gave in was a loud thump and a loud cry, a man's voice.

Leave her alone! was what she thought she'd heard, but she didn't know if the voice was real or imaginary, if it was a human being calling out in her defense or a figment of her imagination. Then the hands that grabbed her suddenly let go and she felt her head bang against hard concrete. Just before everything went dark she managed to see, from the corner of her eye, her attacker running away. She could not see his face, she could not remember anything about him really, but she did notice one thing: the thin frame, the dark mop of hair, the limp of the man who just happened to be there and chase her attacker away.

When she opened her eyes again she saw faces hovering above hers, two middle-aged women, their eyes wide with worry. One of them spoke into her mobile phone.

"Yes, a woman, a young woman, at the corner of 3rd and Wilson, please send someone quickly!"

Her voice resonated with an echo in Sarah's ears, and it made her head hurt.

"What...?" she tried to say, but everything was spinning around her and she felt like throwing up.

"Don't move," said one of the women, now whispering. "Don't move, we called the police, they said an ambulance will be here in a few moments, you'll be fine..."

"What happened?" Sarah managed to blurt out but the voice that came out did not sound like her own.

"You were attacked," said the second woman, the one who spoke on the phone earlier. "We saw him running away. Did he hurt you? Do you know him?"

Sarah lifted her head slightly and looked at her body lying on the dusty sidewalk, one of her shoes missing. She looked at her hands. Then she looked at her shirt, and she realized with relief that although it was slightly torn and a button was missing, everything else seemed intact. She now felt her left shoulder aching, and her head still hurt, but she didn't feel...she did not feel as if her attacker had done anything really awful to her. Her dance bag was not too far from her, and she tried to sit and reach it.

One of the women passed it to her as the sound of the siren became louder, and a police car screeched to a halt close by. A policewoman jumped out from the passenger door, while the driver, a young man, killed the engine and followed his partner.

"How are you? Don't move. Anything broken? Any pain?" asked the policewoman, and Sarah noticed her kind green eyes. She liked her no-nonsense attitude.

"I think I'm ok," she said and sat up slowly.

"We saw him running away," said one of the women. "It was a young guy, but we didn't see his face, only his back."

They helped Sarah onto her feet, and except for her head, which was still spinning, and her aching shoulder, she seemed to be unharmed.

She patiently answered the policewoman's questions and when the ambulance arrived, she let the paramedic examine her while the policewoman waited nearby. Her partner went back to the vehicle, and was now talking on his radio.

"So what exactly *did* you see? Can you please tell me again?" insisted the policewoman, as her young partner returned, ready to take notes.

The two women looked at each other, as if trying to agree on what they'd seen.

"Well..." started one of them. "We just crossed the street there because we wanted to take a short-cut to the movies and we saw these two men fighting. I think one of them was trying to save her, he pulled the other one off her and then the younger one ran away and the other hurried after him."

"There were two men?" interrupted the young policeman, looking at Sarah.

Sarah hesitated, scratching her head. It didn't hurt as much now.

"I think they were not together," said the woman. "I think the other man was trying to stop him, to prevent him from...from attacking her. And I noticed him limp as he chased the younger guy away."

"Interesting," said the policewoman. "So why didn't he stay behind to help?"

The two women shrugged.

"Maybe he saw us and knew we would help her," offered one of them. "Or maybe he'll come back."

They looked around the street, now full of curious passers-by that gathered around the police car.

"Did anyone else see anything?" called out the policewoman. People shook their heads.

"Please write your contact details here, so we can get in touch if we need to," asked the policewoman, and the women did. They then patted Sarah's shoulder and walked away, talking in excited voices about their adventure.

"Can I go home now?" asked Sarah in a small voice.

"Is there anyone you can call, to come and get you?" the policewoman asked.

"I'll be fine," said Sarah. "I'd just like to go home, please. I'll call my mom and she'll come over."

"Are you sure you don't have any idea who this might be?" asked the policeman, putting his notepad in his pocket.

Sarah shook her head.

"Strange that he didn't take your bag," he said.

"Not if he was interrupted by the other man," said the policewoman.

The policeman shrugged.

"I think I do know a limping man," said Sarah hesitantly. They both looked at her; the policeman took his notepad out again.

Sarah described the man to them, saying how she'd seen him again and again all over town in the past few weeks.

The young policeman wrote everything down and took Sarah's contact details, too.

"We'll be in touch," he said. "Can we give you a ride home?"

"That would be great, thank you," said Sarah.

A week later they dropped by her apartment, to see if anything else had come up.

"We don't have any clues, so far, as to who these men might be," said the policewoman. "But we'll keep on searching, of course. Some of these cases never get resolved, but others do."

Sarah nodded.

"Have you seen the limping man again?" asked the policeman, and Sarah shook her head. She had not seen the man again since the incident the previous week. Somehow, she had the feeling she might not ever see him again, but she could not explain why.

"Well, sounds like he happened to be at the right place, at the right time," said the policewoman.

Sarah nodded again, weighing her words. If she were to say what she really thought, they'd think she was out of her mind.

"I think you're right," she finally said. "I think he simply happened to be at the right place."

But she knew she'd keep looking for him in the years to come.

The Year Spring Turned into Winter

It was the year spring turned into winter. The harsh, fast-falling snowflakes surprised the primroses and daffodils that stuck their fragile heads out, ready for the promise of warmth and sunshine.

That same year, ten thousand wildebeest drowned in the Mara River during their annual migration; the same river they, and their forefathers, had been crossing for centuries.

I walked out onto the late March evening to see the full moon shining its ethereal blue light on the snowy fields that only yesterday were covered with spring flowers.

After the evening walk, I came back into the warm house. The logs in the fireplace were still red-hot, sizzling with the passion that I used to feel and could no longer remember. Since you left my life, the passion turned into long quiet afternoons by my typewriter, trying to describe moments that I once lived and were slowly but surely evaporating from my memory.

"My life is my own, you once said to me. I knew you were wrong but did not want to contradict you. For no one's life is entirely their own, and even the most powerful do not know what tomorrow has in store for them.

I heard the knock, but did not get up from my place by the fire, for I was used to hearing voices. Voices in my mind, voices in the night, voices as I awoke in the morning and got myself ready for another day that held little surprise.

But that year, when spring turned into winter, was also the year when my life turned inside out and upside down; for you may think that these words were written by an old woman. But no. Despite my years, I am not old. I am merely beginning my journey. And my journey is tied to yours in knots you could not begin to understand, at least not back then.

The knocking persisted, and finally I got to my feet, and walked slowly towards the door. It was half past nine, an hour when neighbors do not call unless in trouble. Friends stopped knocking on my door some years ago, and enemies did not dare knock, for they sensed the power of what I was becoming and chose other victims to harm; victims who could not harm them.

I opened the door and you stood there in your winter coat, the same one you wore the last time I saw you, many winters ago. You looked older than I remembered. You must be in your seventies now.

"Come in," I said and opened the door, as if it was only natural that a man I had not seen in years would make this nocturnal appearance at my doorstep, in the same night spring turned into winter.

You looked as if you had a speech prepared; something to explain your inexplicable presence on my doorstep. But you did not need to explain, for I knew you would come. I did not know when, but I waited nonetheless.

"I need to talk to you," you said, slightly worried. For you noticed that I hadn't changed since you last saw me all those years ago; if anything, I looked younger.

I sat you by the fire and brought you a glass of port. You accepted it with gratitude and warmed your feet at the flickering flames. The fire grew wilder, as if an unfelt breeze had blown life into it, as it were ready to wither. You were the breeze. You, and no other.

"You don't look surprised," you said – and all I could do was smile. For it was obvious that you would come one day. And why wouldn't you?

When we first met, I was in my thirties; you were in your sixties. I came to you, asking you to let me into your life. Of course I couldn't say why. You were amused at first. Then the amusement turned into fear. I accepted your decision silently, just like I accepted all the other decisions in your life all those years ago.

You did not know who I was, and I preferred to leave it that way, for those who can remember, cannot help those who don't. We have to give you the necessary time, however long that time may be.

I waited to hear what it was that you wanted to say to me, what it was that made you come in the snow and the frost on that one evening. But you remained silent. For even if you knew why you were there, you did not have the words to express it. You were always a man of action, a man of few words, and you were mine, for it is I who brought you into this world and I who taught you what you knew in your first years.

Then you grew up and left home, and I was left to worry, during all those long trips around the world. You risked your life more than once, knowingly, so humanity could learn one more thing about itself, but all that time I had your answers, the answers which you did not wish to hear.

And now you and I, just the two of us, in front of the burning logs. Both of us looked for the right words, which neither of us could find.

"I'd better go," you said after a few moments of silence. "I shouldn't have come."

"So why did you?" I asked and did not have to wait for the answer, for I knew it, like I knew your hands, which have saved so many lives. For it was the same hands that I held during nights you had a fever or a bad dream and asked me to stay by your side, and of course, I did, as any loving mother would.

Now you've come to me for advice, advice that I cannot give you. For the truth is beyond words, it is an entirely different dimension – and if you don't allow yourself to live that different dimension, you will have to live another life. And another, and another, until you do.

You stood up, finishing your glass of port, and put it down by the fireplace. You looked around for your coat, and when I handed it to you, you said, "Thank you, Mother," and suddenly the truth hit you in a place you didn't know existed and you wanted to apologize but couldn't utter the words.

I put my hand on your head, the first time since you were twenty-five and I left you to look after yourself in this world, this world that is just an image. And you understood, and you promised to return.

But you didn't, for the night the spring turned into winter was your last night in this life, and you came to me because on one level or another, you knew.

And the year ten thousand wildebeest drowned in the Mara river, was the same year I began to get old again, just like everyone else. And although I still looked young, I was really one thousand years old. Old enough to rest in peace, like the ten thousand wildebeest that drowned in the Mara River, the year spring turned into winter.

Collecting Feathers

Iopened my front door one late afternoon and looked up at the early-evening skies of autumn. As I stepped out and took a breath of the same air that I had breathed every evening for nearly a century now, it felt different. It was thicker and more damp, with a distinct smell of sulfur. It carried a heaviness that was not usual in our parts. I heard on my short-wave radio that a nuclear reactor had melted thousands of miles away, and I thought: *This might be it*. And still, as if nothing of importance might happen soon, I took my cane and my basket – the same basket I carried for so many years now – and lightly shut the door behind me.

An hour later it started. A stream of long-faced people – entire families carrying their worldly possessions on their backs – arrived in our town as if pulled by an invisible force. They filled the hotels and lodges; they put out their tents at the foot of our mountain and covered our fields with blankets of canvas and plastic and metal. Their voices penetrated through my thin glass windows. Their lights and their worried whispers kept me awake all night.

This was the day for which I, and my mother before me and her mother before her, had been collecting feathers.

The year had been like no other, for the planet shook with rage and spat enormous waves of water that covered villages and towns and even entire cities. When the earth trembled and the seas rose in fury, people stared at their screens in disbelief.

"This is the closest the moon has been to the earth in the last few decades," whispered scientists that month of March, their lips trembling with awe. They checked their measuring equipment, for fear it had been damaged, but when the sun of the nineteenth had set, the full moon glowed in a light that left no room for doubt, for it had never before been so bright, so glorious, so perfectly white.

A fourth moon was discovered that same year. It was observed using the Hubble Space Telescope, circling the icy dwarf planet known as Pluto – three billion miles from earth. It was given the temporary name of P4. But we should have been more worried about our own, single moon, for it is the only one we have.

"The moon is at perigee," I heard an expert explain on my short-wave radio. "There is more gravitational pull, creating higher tides."

I've always kept my short-wave radio nearby – even when others exchanged theirs for more sophisticated electronic equipment half a century before. They all had computers now, and flat-screen television sets and elaborate communication systems. The short-wave radio was a gift to my mother from her own mother; a special gift for the birth of my mother's only child – me.

My mother told me how radio had been invented by a man called Marconi.

"He was a very important person," she said. She told me that different waves exist all around us, even if we humans are unaware of most of them, for they exist in different frequencies from those our own human bodies operate in.

"Some people can tune in to some of these different frequencies," said my mother. "I can, and I will teach you, just like my mother taught me."

"Why, Mama?" I asked, for I really didn't know back then. "Why do we need to tune in to these invisible waves?"

My mother smiled mysteriously.

"It is all about communication – with each other, and with the world beyond the one in which we presently live," she said.

Ten days before the spring equinox, I heard on my radio that a big island had been covered by the Pacific Ocean. Thousands of souls perished and houses, even entire buildings, were reduced to floating rubble. One of the biggest tremors the earth had known in modern times, followed by over two hundred angry aftershocks, and still, the message to people was not clear, not clear enough.

Ten more tremors shook the earth that year, and humans watched helplessly as our planet announced its distress.

The one place spared from natural disasters, even when those disasters multiplied over the globe like cancerous cells in an unsuspecting body, was my town. It was a small and faraway town where people worked hard but enjoyed their rest when the long hours of labor were over. They still greeted each other when passing by on the street, and doors were left unlocked. I was born in this town, and paced its cobbled streets daily at sundown.

I had a job passed down from mother to daughter in my family for at least three generations. It was a duty I've never failed to complete – not one single day since I was eighteen years old, since I took over my mother's duty of collecting the feathers.

The peculiarity of my small town was mentioned in guidebooks and quoted in articles worldwide: an unusually large number of feathers floating in the air, feathers that were white and grey and shimmered with the glitter of dusk and the lightness of the evening breeze, which always came from the north, from the sea. Scientists had researched this unusual phenomenon, and came up with only vague answers.

These were feathers unlike any they had seen before.

"Perhaps they are feathers from the wings of angels." One of them cracked a joke during a debate I listened to on my radio. The others laughed.

I had a large room full of them, a converted barn which has been padlocked for decades. As a child I used to stand in front of the locked door and imagine the angels hiding inside, whispering secrets to each other. When I turned eleven and was allowed to help my mother with the collection of the feathers, she let me go in there once. The barn smelled of lavender and had an otherworldly sensation of weightlessness; walking into it was like walking into a dream. I couldn't see the angels, although I thought I could feel their presence.

When my mother died, I continued collecting the feathers that kept falling on our town from the early-night skies. And now that I knew that the day had come, I was ready for it.

I unlocked the door to the barn—the only locked door in our entire town—and looked down at my long nightgown and my bare feet. They were as old and wrinkled as the branches of the blackthorn tree outside my bedroom window. Its leaves always turned yellow in autumn and fell off in winter, leaving behind a twisted black skeleton. But in spring it was always ready to bloom again, its thin rounded blossoms with their toothed edges eager to hang on the branches in a new cycle of rebirth and of life.

I pushed the heavy door open and a solid mass of feathers inched towards me in the dark, as if it could sense its time has come. A sweet and musty smell drifted in my direction in an invisible wave, covering me like a warm blanket. I could feel my mother's presence right there, next to me. And I thought that perhaps, only perhaps, I could also see an angel standing between the feathers.

I closed my eyes, preparing my skin for the soft touch of the feathers, some of them a century old. They floated around me, caressing my wrinkled skin that had not been caressed for many years, and I waved my arms and pushed them out of the barn. Stumbling in the dark, I fell on my knees, but the feathers continued drifting, as if a gust of wind came out of nowhere and pushed them past me, out through the open door and into the street, into the breaking dawn.

I collapsed on the ground, looking for the angel I thought I saw somewhere inside the barn, before I was able to get up on my feet again. I slowly walked out, my bare feet covered in particles of feathers, my hair wild and my eyes full of tears. I was not crying for myself, for I had no one left in this world, no one who would miss me. I was crying for all these people outside, with their colorful tents and their desperate attempt to escape something that mankind had created without thought of the future.

"It's the feather lady!" cried the town children through foggy windows, and I couldn't understand why they were all awake at dawn. But they opened their front doors and ran outside dressed in their colorful pajamas, small slippers and fleece dressing-gowns, and followed the clusters of feathers that now drifted across our streets with a life of their own.

The guests in our town opened the flaps of their tents and the windows of their stuffy motel rooms and looked up at the sky, where millions of feathers now floated together in a cloud of white.

They had been awake for a while now, watching with

dread a menacing cloud of grey that had been crawling towards our town, hovering above us like a spaceship of poisonous gas, approaching like a confident animal advancing towards its prey. Now they watched as the silvery-white feathers covered the cloud of grey that crawled in, carried on the wings of the northern wind, and they emitted a collective gasp. For they knew that the cloud of grey was their worst nightmare, the one they ran away from, hoping to hide from its toxic fumes and its long-term perils.

I felt exhilaration taking over my aged body as my cloud of white hovered over the grey and surrounded it like the arms of a mother caressing an infant, with a promise of tenderness and love. And the grey cloud, not able to withstand that promise of love, surrendered to the white one. It let the white cloud carry it away, as the northern wind sharply turned south, covering our streets with papers and photographs it had stolen from the homes of those who stared at the clouds, gaping, forgetting to close their doors and windows.

"The feather lady, the feather lady," whispered the adults as I stepped into the wind in my nightgown, my feet heavy with feathers and with age, as I waved my arms at my cloud of feathers and encouraged it southwards, southwards, over the ocean and up into the atmosphere, away from our world.

And I suddenly felt as light as a breeze, lighter than I have ever felt in my long life, and realized that I was floating alongside my cloud, carrying the toxic waste away. Where I was heading I did not know, but I knew that it was the right thing to do, the only thing for me to do, for it would save these people below me and I would be able to rest in peace.

All the years of wondering whether I was communicating with another world or if I had a distorted imagination ended. I realized with relief that I had been doing the right thing all along, even if all those around me did not hear the different frequencies, did not believe that they were real.

I looked down and saw the body of an old woman in a long nightgown lying on the ground by the path to a crumbling barn, its door flapping open and closed with the gusts of wind. I then knew that my duty was done, my task in this life accomplished.

And then I saw the angels. Hundreds of them.

They were all floating beside me over the town, surrounding the toxic grey cloud with their powerful wings, their feathers shimmering in the rising sun like a wall of white gold.

Acknowledgements

Putting a collection of short stories together can be a complex operation, as it involves mixing stories from different genres and different periods in the writer's life. Yet, it is a process that can construct a whole, which is larger than the sum of its pieces, like a sculpture made out of many different pieces of rock.

I wish to thank the following publications and associations for awards and for encouragement over the past decade – awards and encouragement that have kept me going down the writing path even when it was challenging:

The Geneva Writers' Group (*Clockworks* previously published in Offshoots 10, Writing from Geneva, 2009) for inspiration and friendships

The Geneva Times (*Clockworks* reprinted in July/August 2009 issue)

Tonto Books (*The Day of the Dead* first published in More Tonto Short Stories, 2007)

The UK Society of Authors for the John C Laurence Award in 2010

The UK Society of Women Writers and Journalists for awarding *Gemmi Travelers* the first prize in their 2010 overseas Short Story Competition, and for ongoing support and inspiration

The Neil Gunn Trust, Scotland for awards, friendship and inspiration

Swanwick Writers Summer School, UK for friendships and great times

The First Day for publishing *Collecting Feathers* in their spring 2014 issue and editor Jana Llewellyn for wonderful suggestions, including the title of this collection

There are many people who inspired me and who continue to inspire me – on this side of life, and on the other. I am grateful to them all.

My mentor and friend Susan Tiberghien, and the four awesome writing divas: Katie Hayoz, Jawahara Saidullah, Paula Read and Amanda Callendrier. Your feedback is always invaluable. Thank you for your company on my journey.

The dear late Swanwick writers and friends Jean Currie, Roy York and Jackie Cooper – hope you're having a great time together. I know you are cheering for me along the way.

Literary agents Genevieve Carden, Jane Dystel and Miriam Goderich – I feel very fortunate to have you on my side.

My inspiring publisher John Hunt and his great team – Alice Grist, Dominic C. James, Maria Barry, Trevor Greenfield, Nick Welch, Stuart Davies and Mary Flatt – thank you for believing in this book, and for doing something so innovative and forward-thinking with John Hunt Publishing. Working with you is a pleasure and a privilege.

And last, but certainly not least, my wonderful family for their on-going support and for putting up with my writerly anomalies and the strange hours I keep.

Also by Daniela I. Norris

On Dragonfly Wings – a skeptic's journey to mediumship

Paperback 978-1-78279-512-4
$16.95 I £9.99
eBook 978-1-78279-511-7
$9.99 I £6.99

Also from John Hunt Publishing

The Reiki Man
Dominic C. James
January 28 2011 Paperback 978-1-84694-413-0

Scorpio Moons
Helen Noble
August 29 2014 Paperback 978-1-78279-566-7

Without Fear of Falling
Danielle Boonstra
April 26 2013 Paperback 978-1-78099-788-9

Soul Rocks is a fresh list that takes the search for soul and spirit mainstream. Chick-lit, young adult, cult, fashionable fiction & non-fiction with a fierce twist